THE RAVEN'S
SECRET

THE RAVEN'S
SECRET

A Cultural Time Travel Series

RAE JUDY

THE RAVEN'S SECRET
A CULTURAL TIME TRAVEL SERIES

iUniverse books may be ordered through booksellers or by contacting:

iUniverse
1663 Liberty Drive
Bloomington, IN 47403
www.iuniverse.com
844-349-9409

ISBN: 978-1-6632-1012-8 (sc)
ISBN: 978-1-6632-1013-5 (e)

Print information available on the last page.

iUniverse rev. date: 10/14/2020

For my family.

Cultural differences should not separate us from each other, but rather cultural diversity brings a collective strength that can benefit all of humanity.
- Robert Alan

PREFACE

It was during one of my weekly phone calls home to my family that I casually mentioned the story idea. "Cultural objects that allow you to travel back in time, to the place and people where the object came from," I explained.

"Why don't you do it?" asked my dad. He had the habit of asking these types of questions. You know, the seemingly obvious ones that no one else actually thinks to ask. "Write a children's book!" he continued, as if it were the most logical thing to do. And perhaps, it was. And so, it began.

In a land now far, far away – on the west coast of Africa – to the west coast of Canada, the story went from idea to action. I enrolled in a series of online Indigenous world view courses and started reading books on First Nations culture and by First Nation authors. Once relocated to Canada, and to the Comox Valley, I took an introductory lecture series on Northwest Coast First Nations Art through a local gallery. I coupled this with research at the local Courtenay Museum, several trips to the K'omoks First Nations Big House, a Kwak'wala language course at the local library and attended writers' workshops on Indigenous storytelling and cultural appropriation by a local hereditary chief.

Writing about a culture that is not one's own can be a scary act. It's also one that comes with responsibility. Within the pages that follow, I do not pretend to be an expert on First Nations culture – a culture so rich, deep and diverse that its very complexity across time and place can fill countless books and libraries. I admittingly take creative liberties where it suits the narrative flow or interest. For the parts that are historically accurate, I've incorporated them into the Reader Section, to inspire further investigation.

My intent in this story, and the ones that follow in this cultural time travel series, is to instill an interest, respect and curiosity in the minds of its readers to learn more about cultures unlike our own.

We're living in a world of incredible contrast. We are more connected now than ever before, more able to meet and interact with people different from ourselves, and yet, for many, this opportunity is seen as a threat. I strongly believe that stories, even when they are fictional, can help keep our humanity alive by encouraging a curious, rather than antagonistic approach to diversity. By targeting our younger generations and inspiring this type of inquiry, maybe we can all in some small ways help create a more accepting future for us all.

ACKNOWLEDGEMENT

This book was written, in its entirety, on the traditional and unceded territory of the K'omoks First Nation.

There is no way this book would have been completed so quickly if it weren't for my partner, Nicolas. In the early months of being a new mother, he took our son for epic walks so I could blast out any bits of creativity to keep my book idea alive. Not only did he allow me the time and space to do this, but he was also the debut reader of my first draft. As a creative thinker himself, his feedback and perspective played a big role in the unfolding of the words that follow.

I also realized even more benefits to having a literary mother (aside from getting great book recommendations and insightful reviews). Thank you to my amazing Mom who even brought the paper-clipped, A4, draft bundle with her on a tennis vacation to get it done.

My father, as mentioned earlier, was the real catalyst behind getting the ball rolling, or the keyboard flowing. Thank you, Dad, for your endless support and regular 'book update' requests.

To Chief Wedlidi Speck, I am eternally grateful. From the first moment I heard Wedlidi speak in the Kumugwe Big House, I thought "now there is a storyteller!" I am both honoured and deeply grateful that the Chief took time not only to read my draft and provide written feedback, but through his workshops and stories has managed to instill in me a great love for the language, myths and legends that run deep in all aspects of Coast Salish and Kwakwaka'wakw culture. If only more of us could learn the concept of "aweetnakula", I believe our entire planet would be better off.

I'd also like to thank Jeanette Taylor, a local writing instructor, and my entire writers' group who (up until COVID turned our lives upside down) were instrumental in providing feedback across various scenes and helping me kill those evil adverbs!

And finally, thank you to my twelve-year old nephew, Lucas. You are a voracious reader and I took full advantage. Your feedback ("get rid of the emojis" and "you copied the same paragraph twice!") are so appreciated. I owe you more than a breakfast bagel from Mudsharks.

CHAPTER 1

Saira's nose was buried deep in her book when the lady began tapping her shoulder like a woodpecker drumming against a tree trunk.

"Excuse me, dear — are you Saira Amara Lapierre?" asked the airline agent, her square face folding into a frown. "We've been calling you for ages now! Your flight to Comox is leaving."

Saira yanked off her headphones and glanced up from her book, *Great Animal Spirits of the Pacific Northwest.* "Huh?" she said. The beats of Reik, a Mexican trio shared by her best friend Nakawe, came blaring out. "Ugh! I totally didn't hear!"

Racing onto the plane, her backpack bumping up and down on her tiny frame, Saira felt her face burning up. By twelve years old, she'd already been on more planes than most people her parents' age. Now she felt silly. Embarrassed, really. She felt everyone aboard watching as she weaved down the aisle like a salmon frantically swimming upstream.

Safely out of sight and buckled in, Saira closed her eyes and let out a deep sigh. She began nibbling at her fingernails. Ok, so it was her first time traveling alone. Her mom or dad usually told her when it was time to board. It wasn't entirely her fault. But imagine if she'd have missed the plane? What would her Grandpapa think? Saira didn't know him all that well. It had been years since they last saw each other. But she wasn't a kid anymore and she'd be staying with him for two whole weeks. Missing the plane wouldn't be the best start of her trip to Vancouver Island.

1

Pulling out her phone, she saw two unread messages. One from Nakawe: *Sooo jealous!!! TMWU chica*

The other from her mom: *Safe travels, sweetie. Say hi to Grandpapa and see you soon. We love you. xo Mom and Dad*

Saira giggled silently at Nakawe's text. "TMWU" was what Nakawe had started texting when Saira and her mom left Mexico to return to Canada two years ago. She quickly messaged back: *Don't worry, Nak, I'll send mucho pics!*

Saira began biting the side of her lip as she stared back at her mom's text. *Delete.*

Across the aisle came a roar of laughter. There were two kids, around Saira's age, and a man and woman, likely their mom and dad. The mom was pretending to be mad. One of the kids gave her a tickle, then they all burst out laughing. Saira swallowed hard and turned away.

The steward's voice came on over the intercom. Saira normally loved this moment. She'd be nestled in her seat, a parent on each side, about to trade in one adventure for another. This time though, the sound of the safety instructions was twisting the divorce knot in her belly even deeper. She told her counsellor she thought knots were supposed to be good; that they kept things tight and together. Now she realized knots could also mean tough and hard to undo. Saira pulled her headphones over her ears and reached down for her book.

On the inside cover was a handwritten note: *May the animal spirit live on in us all.* She ran her fingers back and forth over the inscription. It was signed *Grandpapa* with the name *Rinaldo Acosta, Ph.D* typed below. It was funny to read a book written by someone she knew, let alone her mom's dad. And even though it was a young person's guidebook on symbols, it made Saira feel very grown-up to be reading something written by "a Ph.D".

"That means he's a doctor," her dad had explained. Ren became Rinaldo's nickname after his family migrated to Canada from Portugal when he was a boy.

Saira was sitting in the back seat of her parents' Volkswagen van when he said this. They were headed to the airport. The book was her going-away present.

"He is not a *medical* doctor, Greg," her mom snapped, shooting Saira's dad a sharp glare across the console. "He's an expert in anthropology — *cultural* anthropology," she continued spitting out the 'c' like it was a bitter tasting berry.

Saira understood what anthropology was. Both her parents were anthropologists too. It meant they studied people and cultures.

Grandpapa was a really big deal in that world. When Saira googled his name, tons of results popped up. He had been a professor at Columbia University in New York City. That's where he met his wife, Saira's grandma. She knew basically nothing about her grandma other than she got very sick, then her and Grandpapa moved back to Vancouver Island, where she was from.

"Grandpapa studied the hidden meanings in objects, animals, dances and songs…even art and magic," Saira's mom explained one day. "He used these meanings and beliefs to help people when they were sick."

This confused Saira. Whenever she got sick, her mom gave her medicine, like aspirins or that terrible purple cough syrup that made her gag.

"Any questions you have, you can ask Grandpapa," her mom said in her telephone voice. This was the tone she used when she was upset or talking with strangers.

Saira snapped out of her daydream. The plane was positioning itself on the runway. She picked up her book and turned to the page where she'd left off. A single red envelope slipped onto her lap. *Another letter from Mom,* she thought.

Red was her mom's favourite colour. "It means life and sacrifice", she used to say. Saira didn't see how a colour could mean these things. Saira reached down to grab the envelope. Her mom often tucked small notes or little trinkets, like colourful rocks or shiny feathers, in her daughter's backpack, lunch bag or jacket pocket. She even made her own stationary with different animal crests sketched along the bottom. Saira loved seeing her mom's designs. But even that wasn't enough to make her open the envelope.

I will not let them divorce, she promised herself. *I don't know how, but I just won't let it happen,* she repeated stuffing the unopened letter back into her bag.

The pilot's voice came on over the intercom. Saira's throat tightened and her eyes started to hurt, like a volcano ready to erupt. The plane engines began to whirr, sending vibrations up into her stomach. She pressed her long black ponytail back into the headrest and pushed her fist deeper into the growing knot in her belly. As she closed her eyes, the plane took off with a sudden jolt into the pale blue Montreal skyline, the contrails behind them fading like a two-headed snake swirling in the wind.

———◆———

Saira barely recognized Grandpapa as she walked through the automatic doors at the Comox airport. His face had thinned and paled and his nose was much longer and pointier than she remembered. It was starting to curve downwards, like a bird's beak. His black hair, once thick and nicely coifed, now fell over his forehead like limp straw. His belly was also much bigger and bulged over this black cargo pants like an over-inflated balloon. If it weren't for his black bucket hat with the rainbow sash, now faded from the sun, Saira might have walked straight past him.

He whipped off his horn-rimmed glasses and tilted his hat up. "There you are, my little traveller!" he cried. His voice was raspy. *Little traveller* was Grandpapa's nickname for Saira. But it was also an Arabic meaning of her name. She was born in Syria's capital, Damascus, before the war broke out. Her parents were both working there when they had fallen in love — with each other and the language.

"Give me a hug, kiddo," Grandpapa said, leaning down to wrap his lanky arms around her. He stumbled forward a moment before catching his balance. "Woooah, gosh these old bones! Or maybe it's my belly? Haha! Not what I used to be, eh?" he continued with a throaty cough as he gave his stomach a couple of hardy pats.

Saira remembered the last time she had seen it Grandpapa. It was four or five years ago. All she remembered was walking along a trail in Qualicum beach, about an hour's drive from Grandpapa's place in Comox. It was cloudy that day and there was a large white raven flying overhead. Just as Saira went to pick some blackberries, the raven swooped down right in front of her and snapped up a small frog. She could have sworn the raven looked her straight on that day.

Grandpapa seemed very excited when she told him what happened. "Lots of mythical meaning in there," he said with a mischievous grin.

Saira didn't know what *mythical* meant, but she guessed it must be a good thing judging by his excitement.

"How's my favourite granddaughter?" Grandpapa asked, reaching around to take Saira's backpack. She smiled and rolled her eyes. She was his *only* grandchild. "Come on, let's get the rest of your bags and head off. I've got a beautiful salmon ready to grill!"

"Oh, yes!" said Saira rubbing her belly. She loved how Grandpapa prepared the salmon. It was her grandma's recipe, apparently. It was one of only three other things she knew about her: she was an incredible cook; she nearly died when she was a baby from eating some wild flower; and when she did pass away, many decades later, it was from an unknown sickness.

———— • ————

Grandpapa glanced over at Saira as he pulled his white truck out of the airport parking lot. "I'm sorry to hear about what's happening at home," he said. His hazel eyes looked much darker than she remembered, almost black. "That's part of life though, kiddo. People grow — together or apart."

"Meh. Whatever. It's ok," replied Saira, fiddling with the purple friendship bracelet around her wrist. It was a gift from Nakawe. She'd given it to her before she and her mom left Mexico to join her dad back in Montreal. Saira hadn't taken it off since. Purple was her favourite colour. Her mom said it meant power and magic.

Grandpapa rolled the windows down, letting the West Coast breeze rush in. A familiar blend of fir, cedar and algae filled Saira's nostrils. She felt happy to be there. Ever since they had moved back to Montreal, two years ago, her parents were constantly arguing. "You need to be honest with me, Alice. You're searching for something…a sense of belonging…identity…I don't know what it is." This was all she heard her dad say through the muffled bedroom walls. It was their last fight before they told her: "This has nothing to do with you. We love you and we are still your parents. But families can change and evolve."

Saira was not interested in her family changing. Why couldn't they just make up? She felt like it was her mom's fault. She was the one who had all this energy. She was like a little hummingbird who wanted to travel the world, sampling the nectars from different cultures. Saira's dad was, in his own words, "tired of the constant up and go". He was perfectly happy to stay in Montreal and continue teaching at McGill University. Rounding the traffic circle, Saira snapped out of her thoughts.

"Grandpapa, wait!" she said, pointing to an enormous totem pole towering from inside the grassy median. "This looks just like the one in your book."

"Impressive, my little traveller!" he chuckled. "You're right. That's a totem pole from the 1940s. That's back when I was just a few years old. Practically ancient, isn't it?" He veered away from the traffic circle and headed down a leafy side street towards Filberg Park. "You might not remember, but you'll see lots of these poles around town…some are new, some are old. Remember, we're on Puntledge land here."

"Pun-wha?" asked Saira, "I don't really remember. What's that?"

"PUNT-ledge," Grandpapa pronounced slowly. "It's the name of the Vancouver Island Northern Salish people. Remember, there are three different tribal regions here: Coast Salish, where we are; the Nuu-chah-nulth on the west side; and Kwakiutl, just north of us. The First Nations were here first. Though we didn't call them First Nations back then. That was waaaaay before any white folk came around. Those white folks were called the settler population. They came to the Comox Valley in 1862. That's nearly over 160 years ago! But the indigenous people had been here for some 8,000 years before that… We, settlers, changed everything pretty much. Yah… did a lot of bad things…" he continued, his voice trailing off as he turned down a small gravel road. "We'll have lots of time to talk about all this over the next couple weeks. I can see you still have your inquisitive spirit!"

Saira was intrigued. She had learned a bit about the First Nations in her grade six social studies class. She knew there were different groups that lived across the country and some still lived on special areas they called reserves. They also seemed to be very attached to their land, nature and animals — all things Saira loved too. She wanted to learn more about these people. *Maybe I'll even get to meet some of them,* she thought with excitement.

"We're here," said Grandpapa, pulling down the tree-lined driveway towards the back of the house. Slivers of the early evening sun trickled down through the branches, tap-dancing their way across the window shield. "Welcome to my little nest, kiddo!"

Saira looked around. His place was hardly *little*. The backyard was practically a forest of towering red and yellow cedars. They were surrounded by sprawling ferns, elder berry bushes and wild lily of the valley. One cedar was unusually tall. Its entire trunk radiated a gorgeous golden colour. The light cast shimmering halos above its branches, while the needles seemed to glow in rich yellow and green hues. A couple of the branches curved down nearer to the ground. They arched together as if waiting to whisper a secret to a passerby or lean in for a gentle hug. Around the base of the golden cedar were a bunch of ripe blackberry and Oregon grapes bushes. Saira made a mental note she'd come back later for some berries.

Behind the trees and off to the right, she could see what looked like Grandpapa's garden. It was so jumbled and overgrown, she wondered if anything edible was actually growing in there. A heaping pile of soil sat off to the side. Wildflowers and weeds were sprouting up everywhere between there and the garden shed whose roof was starting to sag like a wet cardboard box. What was left of the olive-green paint was now started to curl and peel off like the shaved bark of an aging tree.

Around the front yard, Grandpapa's two-storey house overlooked the bay. The front porch, with its large swing and wooden table, looked so calm and inviting in the evening light. Saira loved being near the water and was starting to feel excited about exploring the area. As she walked up towards the house though, she got this unsettling sensation that someone – or something – was watching her every step from the treetops above.

Saira stretched out across the porch swing after supper. Her stomach was ready to explode. They'd eaten barbecued pacific salmon, fry bread, sautéed seaweed salad and fresh salal berry ice-cream. Off into the distance, on her left, she could see Goose Spit Park. Families were out having a picnic along the shore and kayakers on the water just beyond the wharf dock. Mack Laing Nature Park was behind her where she could hear the faint chorus of crickets and the odd yelp from dogs out on their evening walks. And, directly in front of her, was the Comox Bay. It was glimmering like a freshly cleaned pane of glass. Across the bay was the small seaside community of Royston. She could see the outline of homes and the

Shipwrecks pocking out of the water, just beyond the shoreline. Behind them, up to the right, was Queneesh glacier. Its perfectly white snowcaps sparkled under the final moments of the day's sun. Grandpapa told her the creation story of how it formed, over supper. Saira loved hearing about how the Indigenous people were saved from a relentless flood by a great white whale named Queneesh. It was weird that her mom never spoke of these legends, especially since she grew up here.

"Kiddo," said Grandpapa, his voice cawing through the kitchen window. "Don't forget to let your mom and dad know you arrived. It's late over there now and you know how anxious your mom gets when she doesn't hear from you…"

Saira inched off the bench. "Sure, Grandpapa." She wandered over to the door where she'd left her backpack, right next to her Converse sneakers, and sent off a quick text to her mom: *Arrived. Had salmon 4 supper*

Suddenly, a loud thud came from the back of the house. Saira jumped. *What was that? Grandpapa was way over in the kitchen, wasn't he?*

"Hello?" said Saira, squeaking towards the noise. A slice of light stretched out from a room at the end of the hall. The door was slightly ajar and Saira could see the outline of cardboard boxes lined up against the walls. Some were open, their flaps agape. Others were firmly stacked.

"Is there… is anyone there?"

"Hey!" said a man throwing the door open and hopping out. A long piece of black duck-tape dangled from his elbow. He was short with piercing brown eyes, an olive complexion and long jet-black hair pulled back into a loose ponytail. His smile seemed familiar.

"Didn't mean to scare you? Sorry 'bout that. Dropped a few books in here," he said slamming the cap down on a felt pen and extending his right hand. "I'm Tooan-tuh, your Grandpapa's helper. You can call me Tooan," he continued. "I guess he didn't tell you I was here, did he?"

Saira shook her head. Her could feel her face growing hot. But what was she expecting? A burglar? This was hardly a place where crimes were around every corner. One of the safest places in the world, her mom often said.

"Just finishing up," Tooan said swiping a few loose strands of hair from his face. He looked to be about her parents' age and had a faint scar that cut through his left eyebrow. Behind him was a box labeled *Animal Spirits*. "Interested in mythology? Animals? Or maybe both," he asked, following Saira's gaze.

"Both, I guess," said Saira. "I mean, both my parents are anthropologists and we've lived around the world... I've heard a lot about spirits. I totally love animals. I actually think I get along better with animals than humans," she continued, before realizing she was rambling in front of a complete stranger.

"Exactly the same way," said Tooan, tapping his chest. "What's your favourite?"

"Animal? Frogs of course!" she replied. "I love how different they are all around the world. Did you know there are nearly 5,000 different frog species? I had a pet tree frog when we lived in Mexico. My friend Nakawe and I found him in the forest. But then he ran away, just before we moved. I never had the chance to say goodbye..."

"Saira?" called Grandpapa from down the hall. "There you are. I guess you two have met then?" he said from the doorway, shooting Tooan a tight smile. "That'll be enough for tonight, Tooan. Saira, it's late, my little traveller. Time to get ready for bed, then we can take our trip around the world."

As they turned to leave the room, Saira's shoulder brushed up against a long cord nailed to the wall. At the end was a lone golden key that sparkled as she walked by.

Global hopscotch was one of Saira's favourite games of all time. She'd played it with Grandpapa every time they were together.

After randomly choosing a place from his enormous atlas, he would then tell her a story about the people, culture or myths from that place. He had been to so many far-off lands that it was hard to find somewhere he didn't actually know. He had more artifacts than Sarai had ever seen outside a museum. She loved hearing the tales of where these objects came from, what they were used for and who used them.

Sarai plopped herself down onto the living room sofa and nestled herself under an old wooly Chilkat blanket. She heaved the atlas off the coffee table and stretched the book covers open wide. When she opened her eyes, her chewed up fingernail was pointed straight atop northern Brazil.

"Excelente!" said Grandpapa, in a pretend Portugese accent. He pushed himself up off the couch. "Venha," he continued, indicating for Saira to follow.

They walked past the stacked boxes in the hallway towards the room opposite where she'd met Tooan. This was Grandpapa's office. He pulled out a small key from his side pocket and unlocked the door. Saira felt a tinge of excitement as the door hinges quietly creaked open. She'd only been in once before and entering this room was like walking into an entirely new world. A warm, pungent smell of sweetgrass, sage, tobacco and dust bunnies tickled her nose. The air felt hot and thick. There was just enough light streaming in from the hall to see the outline of a towering glass cabinet, a couple of wooden bookshelves and a giant desk overlooking his garden. Grandpapa switched on a floor lamp with the click of his foot. Saira looked carefully around the room. Her gaze finally rested at his desk. What a disaster! Heaps of crumpled papers, tattered old books, mounds of different coloured notepads, an assortment of pens, a desk light and a single bronze paper weight were all thrown across the top. The windows above his desk were covered with long and wrinkly sun-bleached, brown, linen curtains. Saira walked over to the cabinet and with her fingers smeared away lines of dust coating the glass. Inside were some tiny colourful wooden masks, a couple of bronze figurines and various sizes of brown and black leather-bound books. Grandpapa tugged the cabinet door open and took out a small, red pouch from behind an unidentifiable carved wooden disk.

"Here, my little traveller," he said, pushing his glasses up. He delicately opened the satchel, his fingers trembling slightly. "I know you learned a bit of Spanish when you lived in Mexico. The name of these is very similar in Portuguese..."

He turned the bag upside down and gave it a couple of shakes. Out fell a small polished stone. It had a smooth and glossy black finish and was about five centimetres long. It was curved like a baby snake with two heads and had a small hole drilled through one end with a long and heavily frayed piece of brown leather string.

"This here is a pedra encantada — that's Portuguese — or piedra encantada in Spanish," he continued, emphasizing the "i". His face took on a strange glow.

Sarai put one hand out to touch the cold, glassy surface and paused. "Umm...enchanted stone?" she asked, twiddling a strand of hair.

"Good!" he laughed. "When I was working with the Yagua shamans in the Upper Amazon — that's in Brazil — they gave me this, and a few other rocks, as souvenirs. You wear it like this," he continued, wrapping the leather strap around Sarai's neck. "The leather is a bit old now so you might want to keep it in this medicine pouch instead. The pouch is traditionally from our Native American neighbours, down south."

Sarai's mouth went round like a saucer and a small chill crept up her back. "Cool! Is the stone magic? Like, does it have... *special* powers?"

"Course not," he answered in delight. "The spirits have long since left...probably moved on to other stones. This one is unique though, because of its shape and colour," he said tracing his finger along the curled stone.

He paused for a few seconds, lost in thought.

"I'm getting on in years now. I'm going through my stuff and, well, now it's yours. You can tell all your friends back in Montreal that you have yourself a genuine *pedra encantada!*" he continued, gently leading her out of the office. "Ok, my little traveller, hop to it! It's getting late. We'll talk more about it tomorrow."

Before Sarai crawled into bed, she sent Nakawe a text and picture of her new stone: *Check it out, Nak! Got magic rock from Grandpapa!! Do you know these? I want to wake the spirits!!*

After sending the message, she realized Nakawe would probably feel jealous. But at the same time, she was pretty sure Nakawe might know about these rocks. She was a Yaqui, born and raised in a village outside Mazamitla, in the Sierra Madre mountains of Mexico. Her people believed in the existence of many different worlds.

That night, Saira tossed and turned in bed. She kicked the covers and rearranged the pillows countless times. She couldn't stop thinking about her parents' divorce and the magic stone. *What if… what…if? What if these spirits could help me?* She began rubbing it softly as her mind raced. The lump in her throat grew tighter. *How can I get them to stay together?*

Laying there in the dark, she remembered it was the first time she'd been alone at Grandpapa's without her parents. She pulled the duvet up snug around her neck and grabbed the stone off the bedside table clutching it in her palms. *Spirits are you there? You can't just disappear…I will get this magic stone to work.*

Outside the sound of the wind blowing through the tall cedar trees grew louder. Saira clenched her eyelids shut and after a couple hours finally drifted off into a deep slumber, the stone falling gently from her fingers onto the cedar floorboards below.

CHAPTER 2

Saira dreamed she was swimming effortlessly through a mysterious cold liquid. All around her were iridescent shades of blue, green and purple that swirled and transformed like an underwater kaleidoscope. A long, red and black blanket covered her entire body. In her teeth, she clenched the magic stone. Up and down, she moved gracefully passing other shapes and colours. There were spiky pinks; long, spindly greens; white ovals; and flecks of gold that danced before her. She felt safe, even though nothing was familiar. It smelled of sand and salt, laced with a hint of seaweed and cedar.

Above the water, Saira saw the blurred outlines of giant red and yellow cedars, Douglas firs and spruce trees. They swayed to the movement of the wind and towered under a magnificent blue sky speckled with puffy mounds of white. Saira lept up, as if to touch the cotton ball clouds, then dove back down into the mirage of hues. A rush of energy washed over her. From a distance, she heard muffled voices. They were growing closer.

Mom and Dad! she thought, as she swam forward. *They're coming to tell me they made a huge mistake. They are not separating after all.* Saira sped even faster towards the voices. She could see two figures walking single file up along the shore. The first one bounced along the trail. It had a long, pointed nose, small feet and was holding a bouquet of flowers in one hand. The second figure was hopping along behind, trying desperately to keep up. It had much shorter legs, webbed hands and was carrying a large coiled cedar bark basket. In the background, Saira heard the steady sound of drums. The beat was pierced by a loud shriek, then from out of nowhere a massive bird swooped down from the sky like a fighter jet, its thick, black neck and long, wedge-shaped tail poised for attack. It lunged at the figures. The knife of its beak dove straight for the head of the person carrying the basket and then, just as suddenly, the bird swooped back up with amazing strength, carrying the newfound prey in his talons.

Saira woke with a start. Her pajamas were stuck to her body and her throat hurt.

Wow, what a crazy dream. So strange. It seemed so real… she thought, rubbing her face. She looked around the room. *But… but my parents are not back together and I'm still here in Comox by myself,* she remembered.

Saira peered down and, under the morning light, saw the outline of the leather string and magic stone sitting undisturbed on the floor. She reached down and began rubbing it with her thumb. *Come on, spirits! Are you in there or not?* she whispered.

The beeping sound from her phone interrupted her thoughts. Two new messages: one from her mom: *Thanks for letting us know, sweetie. I hope you are having fun so far? How's Grandpapa? We love you. xo Mom and Dad*

The other from Nakawe: *So cool @piedra encantada! They r soooo rare!! Spirits love tobacco. TTUL*

Tobacco!? Hmm…. Saira thought to herself, as she jumped from bed. *Grandpapa must have some around the house somewhere!* She pulled the leather string around her neck, tucked the magic stone under her housecoat and headed for the kitchen.

"Morn, kiddo," chirped Grandpapa, intersecting her at the stairs. A tattered apron was wrapped around his waist, the frayed ties dangling to one side. Specks of flour splattered across his cheeks and through his hair. "Sleep well?" he continued with a gruff cough. "Ahh, damn cough… s'cuse me a moment," he continued, pivoting back around towards the kitchen. He hacked a few more times, before shooting back a couple of pills with a slurp of water.

"Grandpapa, you don't sound well at all," said Saira, following closely behind him. "You sound really sick."

"Nah, just a pesky cold, that's all," he replied, clearing his throat and throwing another piece of fry dough onto a crackling pan. Specks of oil shot up onto the counter narrowly missing his forearms. "Damn thing is too hot! I'm just fixing us some breakfast. A hearty local breakfast. I call it my Coastal Salish Special!"

"Yum," Saira said, before adding, "Grandpapa, do you have any cigarettes?"

"Ciga—? What? You're about 20 years too long to be smoking, young lady," he said, wiping his hands up and down on his apron before flipping the fry bread over with expert finesse.

"No, no, Grandpapa. I just want to try feeding my stone some tobacco. You know, to maybe awaken the spirits," Saira replied, turning her head away.

"Ha, my little traveller! You really are a curious one, aren't you? I see you've already done some research. Here, take my key and go to the office."

Grandpapa pulled the key ring from his cargo pant pocket, passing it to Saira. "Don't muck around in there though! It might look like a mess, but it's my *organized* mess. Just take the smudge stick off the windowsill. It's on the pink abalone shell. There's tobacco in those sacred herbs." She was already speeding towards the hall. "But, don't get your hopes up!" he continued, his voice trailing off. "Those spirits have long since gone…"

Saira didn't care if the spirits had gone. She was eager to try it out anyway.

In the morning light she was amazed to see how cluttered Grandpapa's office actually was. Even the walls were covered. Photos were everywhere. Some were nicely framed and hung in straight lines along the wall. Others weren't photographs at all, but certificates and degrees with shiny deckles and fancy writing. Other photos were loose and scattered randomly on top of his bookshelves, the edges frayed and yellowed. There were photos of Grandpapa in his much younger years, some with Grandma, and some with people Saira didn't recognize but who looked very exotic. There were tall, lanky men whose bodies were painted in beautiful white mud patterns with bones poking through their cheeks and women with dozens of rings spiraling around their long necks and massive labrets protruding from their lower lips. Grandpapa started touring the world after Grandma passed away. He worked in all sorts of places like Zimbabwe, China, Australia and Papua New Guinea. He won his awards from curing people in these places.

Over on the windowsill, Saira spotted the abalone shell and, sure enough, the last bits of a smudge stick. She broke off a pinch and scrunched it against the polished stone. A delicious earthy scent filled her nostrils. She took a deep breath in and closed her eyes. Her heart began to beat faster. *Please work! Please, please, please work,* she whispered into her cupped hand.

Outside, the faint musical sounds of a man's voice came sailing in. Startled, Saira looked down at her magic rock. Nothing. No change at all. But the melody from outside continued and seemed to be growing louder. It sure didn't sound like Grandpapa. Saira pulled back the faded linen curtains. Puffs of dust wafted up her nose, making her sneeze. She then saw Tooan at the very back of the yard. He was standing in the middle of the plot of soil, his armpit resting on a large shovel. Sitting next to him were a couple giant cardboard boxes and some objects strewn at his feet. He was hauling more things out of the boxes and, seemingly, planting them in the ground. *Was he planting them, though? Or…maybe was he burying them?*

"Saira? Saira? Any luck with the stone?" asked Grandpapa from the doorway, his eyebrows slightly furrowed.

Saira was looking down at the green and brown herbs scrunched in her hands. "Nah, not so far," she answered. "Maybe they've really left, Grandpapa…That or they're sleeping." She forced a quick smile, then wiped the remaining ashes on her jeans.

"Come on now, kiddo! We can find other ways of finding spirits, if that's what you're looking for," Grandpapa said, tapping Saira's back as he led her out of the room. "Now give me back the key and let's have some breakfast. I have to rush out to an appointment. I'll leave you with Tooan for a bit."

Grandpapa had prepared another massive meal that was spread across the long wooden kitchen table. He passed Saira a plate and pointed out each dish with the end of his fork. "This, here, is wild boar sausage patty. Then, there's fry bread from last night, which I've made into French toast. You can put this local salmonberry syrup on it or go for the Salish herbal explosion jam," he continued.

"Great," said Saira feeling her belly rumble. She picked up the mason jar with bright purple contents. "What's this explosion jam?"

"A long-standing family secret. Recipe goes back generations…" he replied grinning.

"Aww, Grandpapa! It can't be a family secret if Mom doesn't know it… not that she cooks anything anyway," Saira said under her breath.

"Why don't I show you while you're here then? But for now, I'll tell you there are many types of local berries, some hibiscus flowers and two other mystery ingredients."

Saira slapped a spoonful onto her plate. She grabbed a couple pieces of the fry bread French toast and sausage and walked out to the porch. No sooner had she sat down than a small white dog came bounding up the stairs. Its long, pink tongue dangled from the side of his mouth as it lunged for her plate like a baseball player stealing for home base.

"Woooah!" cried Saira, yanking her plate back, the sausage nearly tumbling to her lap.

"'Wat'si! 'Wat'si! Stop that, get down!" Tooan yelled. "Sorry 'bout that Saira. Rambunctious one, he is! Still a pup."

"He's so cute," said Saira, nestling his long, soft undercoat. "What kind of dog is he?"

"A spitz-retriever mix. His ancestors, way back over a hundred years, are actually Coastal Salish wool dogs, but they're long since extinct," explained Tooan. "At one time, the First Nations people actually used the wooly dogs to make Salish blankets instead of sheep's wool... His name, 'Wat'si, means "dog" in Kwak'wala. That's my native tongue, on my mom's side," he continued.

"Cool," replied Saira, picking up the bit of sausage. "Can I give him some?"

Tooan crouched down on the veranda steps. "Just a bite. He's got a big appetite, especially for that tasty salmon your Grandpapa cooks up. I can hardly get enough of it myself!"

Just then Grandpapa stepped out onto the porch, a takeaway coffee mug in one hand, his briefcase in the other. "Heading out now," he said, wiping the last bits of fry bread from his mouth. "Shouldn't be long. Saira, maybe Tooan will let you take 'Wat'si out for a walk down by the water? That way Tooan, you can finish up with the... ah... gardening and other stuff. Just be careful down there, Saira. Watch where you're walking, eh?"

"Good idea," replied Tooan, ruffling 'Wat'si's head. "You'd love that now, wouldn't you?"

"Ok, Grandpapa," answered Saira, just as 'Wat'si jumped up to give her a big, slobbery lick across her cheek.

———•———

Saira had faint memories of playing on Grandpapa's property the last time she was here with her Mom and Dad. They went out walking in the forest a lot together. Her mom always whirling along the trails, like a little bird, as she gathered up all the beautiful wildflowers to make a bouquet. She and Saira both loved walking among all the giant firs, elm and cedars, listening to the hum of insects and feeling the cool fresh air on her face.

"Hey, slow down," Saira laughed, as 'Wat'si tugged his leash. After a few minutes, they arrived at a clearing overlooking the bay. It was an idyllic summer morning. Queneesh was sparkling in the sun, the water was still like glass and an eagle was soaring overhead, its wings perfectly reflected in the waters below. Saira pulled on 'Wat'si's leash to stop. She wanted to take a selfie to send to Nakawe: *Outside Grandpapa's house! Wish u were here!*

Nakawe almost replied instantly: *Looks so nice!! TMWU... Sooooo bored here. Any news about tobacco???*

Saira began typing out her response: *I found some, but didn't work. Any other ideas?? Maybe spirits really r gone.*

'Wat'si was starting to get restless and just as Saira was about to press "send" on her text, he bolted from her grasp and began racing towards the water. "'Wat'si! Stooooop!" Saira yelled, scrambling to catch up.

She tore through the fields of dandelion, red elderberry and hedge nettle, the magic stone beating up and down against her collarbone like a metronome. 'Wat'si finally stopped and stuck his nose to the ground. He then began digging frantically in the mud next to a giant patch of dandelions and an enormous salmonberry bush. As Saira got closer, she could see that he was trying to get at a snake that was slithering up a small stump. The poor thing was fleeing for its life! Saira lunged to step onto 'Wat'si's leash, but her foot slipped. Her body lurched forward as she fell directly on top of the log. Her arms splayed out to break her fall and the magic rock hit up against her chin. She felt a sharp jolt followed by a hot, tingling sensation. She saw sharp specks of red and purple dancing in the sky, then everything froze and went black.

CHAPTER 3

Saira woke to the throb of drums and a low hum that sounded like wild rhythmic chanting. Her head ached and her palms burned from the fall. She looked down at her hands, but she couldn't see anything. She lifted her arms, but they were caught on something – something draped over-top, some kind of tarp-like fabric.

"What in the world?" she whispered. She turned her head from side to side until she felt her way towards what seemed like an opening. But then her hands hit up against something cold and hard. It also smelled oddly familiar. A bit earthy, like ashes at a campfire, but she couldn't tell exactly what it was. The sound of the drums and voices was louder, more intense. *What…what happened? Where am I?* Saira's heart starting to beat faster. She tried propping herself up onto her back elbows, but couldn't fully breathe with the thick cloth in her face. Under her t-shirt, she felt the coldness of the magic stone against her collarbone. Then she remembered 'Wat'si. *Oh my gosh, where is he? We were walking… he started running…*

Her mind raced as she tried to recall the last sequence of events. She reached for her cell phone. The screen lit up and she could see there was now a large crack across the front. It read 9:53am. She had no idea what time she left Grandpapa's house, but guessed it wasn't that long ago. She switched on the phone's light and pointed it upwards. She was laying under a dark cloth, but could see a small slit of light where she managed to tug the fabric loose and scramble her way out. There were large wooden beams overhead.

That smell! she realized. *It is so familiar, but where…?* Saira only knew that she was inside somewhere and other people were obviously around, somewhere. She headed for a dark corner and waited for her sight to adjust. A few metres in front she could see a large, white curtain decorated with an enormous spread eagle. There was an opening around the bird's abdomen just big enough for a person to crawl through. She edged closer and peered through. A group of women, draped in red and black blankets with white buttons, twirled around a large burning fire. On their heads were triangular, cedar bark-rimmed hats covering their long black hair. Some women carried wooden rattles, waving them around like wands. Others wore elaborate masks — in green, red, yellow and black —with long, straggly bits of cedar bark hanging down like unruly hair. The bark made light crinkly noises as the masks bobbed up and down to the rhythm of the drums. Saira carefully pulled back the panel a bit further and arched her head towards the ceiling. A single beam of sunlight fell through the rectangular gap in the roof. It was just enough to see the silhouettes of people sitting in a large circle around the dancers. On the other side, Saira could see a dozen or so men seated face to face. They wore colourful vests and thick headbands with large feathers splaying out. They beat down on a large overturned tree trunk with heavy wooden batons that looked like clubs and were singing in low, monotone voices. Small splinters of cedar shot up into the air like confetti and loose bits of feathers gently made their way to the ground like soft, falling snowflakes. All around people were moving slowly as they danced barefoot around the crackling fire.

This is unbelievable, thought Saira. *I need to record this.* No sooner had she pulled out her phone to film that she heard a small voice next to her.

———◆———

"*Yo,*" whispered the young girl.

"Oh!" said Saira, jumping back, her hand on her chest. "Gosh, you scared me!"

"Ha ha, shhhh…sorry," the young girl said, placing a finger over her mouth. A sweet smile quickly spread across her lips. She looked about Saira's age. She had a long and thick black braid falling down her back, friendly eyes and an olive complexion. She was wearing a cedar bark skirt that looked similar to the ruffled hair on the masks. On her feet were ankle-length moccasins laced with beautiful, coloured beads and light brown fur along the rim.

"I thought you might be a… *newcomer*," she said, drawing closer to Saira. "My name is Kwa'akwamta," she said extending her hand. "But everyone on the reserve just calls me Wamta. You?"

"I'm Saira… Sorry, I'm totally confused…reserve? What reserve? Where am I exactly? How did I…? I was just out walking my dog… not *my* dog really… but anyway, he started to run and well I hit my head and now, well, this is all messed up…"

Wamta's smile grew larger.

"What do you mean, 'messed up'? You're funny! But you really shouldn't be here, you know. You've snuck into our secret potlatch and could get in big trouble…. Hey, what's that?" she said, pointing at Saira's phone.

"Sorry, I snuck into your *what*?" asked Saira, ignoring her question about the phone. "Is *that* what's happening here?" she said, pointing to the open room of dancers and chanters.

"Our *potlatch*. Yes, that's what's happening here. It's a Chinook word. It means 'to give'. But honestly, we're not allowed to have them anymore, so you better not be with the government… Wait a minute. Are you??"

"What, me? Government? We're, like, the same age," said Saira, rolling her eyes. "But wait. Is this — *illegal*?"

"I guess I shouldn't expect you to know… They banned our potlatches many, many years ago… We have to organize them in hiding, which is why not everyone is here. And really, we shouldn't even have the music or button blankets…They make too much noise…Speaking of which, here, take this blanket and mask," she continued, passing her a large, navy and red robe and a mask with a long, hooked nose. The robe had a beautiful crest appliqué in red and, what looked like, hundreds of white abalone and mother-of-pearl shells sewn across. "I'm not too sure about those," she said, eyeing her Converse sneakers. "If anyone sees you in them, they'll know you're an outsider. I don't know where you got those, but you might want to take them off?"

"Where have you been?" asked Saira, kicking her shoes off into a dark corner. She then pulled on the robe. It was thick and heavy, and smelt of freshly dried leather and fur. She tried to strap the mask on, but it was so big and wobbly that Wamta had to help sturdy it.

"What are you guys celebrating, anyway?" asked Saira, tilting her head back to see Wamta beneath the mask.

"It's a celebration of life," answered Wamta. Her face grew dim. She gestured towards the cloth Saira had pulled herself from under.

"We're unveiling our new family crest on the carving today."

Saira realized she was pointing towards the large overturned tree trunk.

"The kikw will be put in front of our clan house later. It was carved to honour my brother…"

"Kikw? You mean that totem pole?"

"Yes, kikw is the Coast Salish word," said Wamta. "My dad was Coast Salish and my mom is Kwakwaka'wakw, so I speak a bit of both. I'm from up north, near Alert Bay."

"Cool," said Saira.

"*Cool*?" repeated Wamta.

"Like pretty neat…you know, nice," answered Saira, eyeing her new friend. "So, like, why does he get one, your brother?" she asked, glancing back towards the dancers.

Wamta's voice started to crack, "It's… it's a… kind of memorial. He disappeared four summers ago. We don't really know what happened, but he has never been seen again. When someone dies, we wait four years before putting up the kikw."

Saira looked down. "I'm so sorry. I didn't realize."

"It's OK," replied Wamta. After a few seconds, she continued: "Do you have any siblings?"

"No. Nope. Just me. My parents only wanted me, I guess," said Saira, her voice trailing off before adding, "I always wanted a brother or sister. And now my parents are…well, they're splitting up."

Wamta was just about to reply when they were interrupted by a large, furry, black creature that burst through the front door of the longhouse. It wore a huge mask with big eyes and bright, red lips. Bedraggled hair sprawled out from all sides. She had massive breasts and big, black gloves on her hands and on her back was a large, cedar bark basket. From underneath the mask came a loud "huuuu, huuu" sound.

Wamta grabbed for Saira's hand and pulled her into the centre of the room. "We gotta go! It's nearing the end of our potlatch."

— ◦ —

Saira was mortified. She'd just been flung into the centre of a big dance full of complete strangers. Not only did she have no idea where she was or who she was with, but she had no idea how to move to this type of beat. It wasn't exactly like dancing to Mexican hip hop in her bedroom with Nakawe.

"What *is* this?" whispered Saira, pointing to the terrifying looking animal as it began dancing clockwise around the fire and rubbing its eyes with its oversized gloves. A man was carefully leading the creature with a rattle.

"This is Tsonoqua. Or Tal, in Coast Salish," answered Wamta.

Saira's face contorted "Say what? I don't even know what you just said!"

"Haha, OK. It's a bit hard to pronounce. Just call her our 'Wild Woman of the Woods'," explained Wamta.

She reached for her phone again to snap a photo. She wanted to show Nakawe. She'd never believe this!

"Hey, what are you doing?" hissed Wamta, pushing Saira's hand down and nudging her off to the side.

Saira nearly dropped her phone. "What's with you? Can I *not* take a picture?"

"A picture? With *that*?" Wamta sputtered, pointing to her smartphone.

"Are you, like, actually kidding me?" exclaimed Saira. "Of course, with *this*! You're acting like you've never seen a phone camera or something?" she continued. "Here. I'll show you."

Wamta and Saira scurried to another dark corner of the longhouse. But it was too late. Wamta's grandmother had already spotted them from across the room.

"Oh no! We've got to get out of here! My ada has seen us," she said, shoving Saira towards the door.

* ◆ *

Once outside, the two girls both breathed huge sighs of relief, but each for very different reasons. Wamta knew she'd be in trouble for running out of the dancing circle and Saira was still totally confused about the whole situation. She heaved off the mask then removed the navy and red robe. She needed to find 'Wat'si and get home. Looking up, though, she realized she was nowhere close to home.

Sure, it was the Comox Bay. But the scene was different. The tide was out and she could see long, wooden poles poking out of the water in a type of figure eight configuration. Colourful canoes with wide sterns rested ashore. And to her right, a dozen long and narrow, log houses were neatly lined up facing the water. They all had the same extended, square gabled roofs and large totem poles standing out front. Saira swiveled her head back around and saw that the building where she and Wamta had just left was, in fact, much, much bigger than all the other houses. But more impressively than its size was the gigantic painting on the front door with its large, green and black eyes, flared red nostrils and many teeth. Two carved poles, each towering nearly 20 metres high, stood directly in front.

"What in the world?" Saira whispered under her breath, turning her head back around to the bay. Off in the distance, across the water, she spotted Queneesh. *Phewf!* she thought, before realizing that something there was not right either.

Queneesh's glistening snowcap seemed much, much brighter. After a few seconds, Saira realized the glacier was at least double the size she remembered. It was extending part-way down the mountain! For the first time, the glacier even looked like the profile of a boy sleeping on his back.

Wamta rested her hand on Saira's shoulder. "Are you OK? You have a funny look."

Saira remained silent, focused on the landscape. Her gaze moved downwards, to the left of the glacier.

"What? What — happened to Royston?" she said to no one in particular. "Where are all the homes I saw last night? This — is this some kind of joke?"

"What are you talking about," Wamta asked. "Come on, let's get you changed into something other than those," she continued, pointing to Saira's jeans. "Then we can come back for the kikw raising ceremony and feast."

But Saira wouldn't budge. Her head shot to the left. Along Goose Spit, there were no signs of cars at the beach or motorized boats of any kind. The long wharf dock was there, but otherwise there weren't any other signs of kayakers or any other water sports whatsoever. All there was, was water and so many trees.

Saira's voice started to tremble. "Wamta, I'm going to ask you a very silly question." She felt for the magic stone under her shirt. "What — what *year* is it?"

Wamta let out a laugh and grabbed for Saira's hand. "You really are strange, aren't you? First, you sneak into our potlatch dressed in some kind of strange outfit. Then you pull out an object you call a *phone* that fits in your *pocket* and takes *photos!* And now you are acting like you don't know what year it is!" Wamta continued, leading Saira into one of the plank houses. "It's July 1941, of course. Now, come on!"

For a split second Saira was sure her heart had stopped. She pulled her phone back out of her pocket to check the time. It read 9:53am but the date was missing. She checked her messages. Her reply to Nakawe hadn't sent. She pressed send. *Message failed.* She pressed it again. Nothing. The network symbol in the upper left-hand corner of the screen was searching for a connection. Saira's face paled. "But...how — how did this happen?" She reached for the stone around her neck and brought it up to her face. "Was it you?" she whispered looking down at the glossy stone. It warmed under her touch.

Wamta pulled Saira into one of the rectangular plank buildings. The door was quite small and had a large circular relief carving on the front. It was cool and humid inside and the room stretched out to nearly 30 metres long. The roof was made of long red cedar planks held in place with cedar bark withes and supported by huge beams. The mid-morning sunlight snuck its way through the small cracks in the roof and the square cut-out side windows. The embers from smoldering ashes were glowing from a fire pit and the scent of old wood and herbs seeped into her nostrils. Mats were carefully laid out over the dirt floor – some made of animal hinds, others cedar bark. There were mostly women and children milling about — some tending to the fire with babies strapped to their back, others preparing food as they sorted through baskets of berries.

"This is where we – me and my family – live," explained Wamta, pointing to a small corner of the room. "That's my mom."

Saira could see a mother breastfeeding her young baby behind an upright mat that served as a dividing curtain from the rest of the room. She was reclined on a cedar bark mat with a woolen Hudson's

Bay Company blanket wrapped around the baby. A half-woven, spruce root basket lay next to her along with some random pieces of grass and cat tail.

Wamta walked over. "*Abas*, this is my new friend, Saira," she said. "Saira, this is my abas — that's mother in Kwak'wala — and this is my baby sister. She doesn't have a name yet. She's only eight months. We name our kids at ten months."

"Hi," said Saira, looking at both Wamta's mom and baby sister. "Nice to meet you both."

Wamta's mother offered a warm smile and extended her hand. Like Wamta, she had a long, black braid that reached far down her back and had the same warm skin tone. She wore a beautiful shell necklace that sat loosely on her collarbone and had a friendly, though very tired looking face.

"Wiksas?" her mother asked Saira. "Digilala, kwalayu," she said looking over at Wamta.

Saira looked at Wamta.

"She's asking how you are and telling me to make some tea," she explained smiling and pointing towards the mat.

Saira twirled the thread bracelet around her wrist. "Good question," she said, forcing a laugh. "I'm fine... though totally confused."

"And your family?" Wamta's mom asked with an accent.

Saira felt the divorce knot pinch inside her belly. "They're OK."

"Ikikala," explained Wamta to her mom. "Sorry, she doesn't speak much English. I just told her they were fine," explained Wamta, removing a small wooden bowl from under a cloth.

The bowl was painted on the sides with an elaborate green and red creature with big beady eyes. Wamta then reached into a small a burlap satchel and took out a pinch of dried stinging nettle and liquorice fern root. She sprinkled it into the bowl and poured hot water overtop, stirring it round a few times with a small wooden spoon.

"How do *you* know English then?" asked Saira.

"At school. I go to a mixed school here in Comox. It's great. I love it. But in September I'm starting at the Indian school in Port Alberni. It's where my brother went. The teachers there are from the United Church and, actually, he hated it… He said they don't let you speak our languages and we have to wear uniforms. They don't let us practice any of our culture at all," she said her pupils widening. She extended the wooden bowl of tea to Saira, "Here. You can drink from this bowl. It was my brother's."

"Thank you," said Saira, taking the tea with both hands. But just as her fingers touched the cedar bowl, she felt a light tingly sensation as they started to go numb. The hairs at the back of her neck began to rise up, her heart skipped a few beats, then, just as suddenly, everything went still. Stars shot up into her eyes, her feet started to tremble and the room went black.

CHAPTER 4

Saira woke to 'Wat'si's tongue rolling up her cheek like she was a giant piece of salmon. His leash still dragged behind him in the mud and the snake was nowhere to be found. Rolling over, Saira pushed him away. Long pieces of grass and dandelion leaves flicked at her nose. The cries of eagles shot down from overhead. She blinked, then propped herself up.

"Nooo! Where are my shoes?" Saira cried, looking down at her dirty toes.

"Brrraaa! Brrraaa!"

Saira swung her head back. "Did you? Did you just try...to... *speak* to me, 'Wat'si?" she asked, her gaze narrowing. "That was definitely *not* a bark."

"Brrraaa! Brrraaa!" he answered, his tongue pulsating between his bottom teeth.

"What in the world?" cried Saira, jarring her head back. 'Wat'si pointed his nose off to the side. Just next to where she had fallen, was the wooden bowl and the stump she'd tripped over. There were still bits of wet tea leaves stuck to the bottom. As she placed her fingers in, her phone beeped from her back pocket.

9.58am. Nakawe had sent a reply to Saira's earlier text: *I'll check other ways 2 wake spirits! Imagine if u really had magic powers! TMWU!!*

Saira just stared back at the message. *9.58am? Was I dreaming? What about Wamta, the potlatch, her missing brother and the Wild Woman of the Woods?*

Off in the distance, she could see the swing on Grandpapa's porch. Royston was in front of her, the Comox Bay was just as she remembered and Queneesh was back to the size she'd seen the night before.

Ok, so I'm back home. But where are my shoes? And how did this wooden bowl with tea leaves get here?

She looked down at the magic stone, around her neck. "Are you in there?" she whispered into her cupped hands. "Did you take me back in time?"

Saira reached back for her phone and sent a reply off to Nakawe: *Nak, we gotta talk! U'll never believe what I have 2 tell u…*

Just as she placed her phone back in her pocket, she heard a loud "psssst" from behind. Turning her head, all she could see were the flickering dandelion leaves swaying next to her.

"Pssst! Pssst!" said the voice again.

Saira scrunched her face up and leaned into the grass. The sound seemed to be coming from the leaves. But that was impossible. There was nothing there. *Plants don't talk*, she said to herself, shaking her head.

'Wat'si responded with a *brrraa! brrraaa!* then started chasing a small frog through the long blades of grass.

"Come on, 'Wat'si!" yelled Saira, grabbing for his leash. "We gotta get home, safe, before I lose you again… or something even crazier happens!"

As Saira and 'Wat'si made their way up Grandpapa's porch, she could see Tooan on the balcony. A boy was sitting next to him.

"Quick walk! Everything OK?" Tooan asked, looking down at her muddy feet.

Saira wiggled her toes. "Oh, yah. Sure. I… ah… I kinda left my shoes back down by the water." One hand was rested on her hip, while the other clutched the small wooden bowl behind her back. She wasn't sure why, but she wanted to hide it.

"This my son, Satsam," said Tooan, turning towards the teenage boy. He was sorting through a pail of berries and herbs. He had his dad's same tanned skin and jet-black hair.

"Hi," said Saira waving her hand up.

"S'up," said Satsam, shooting her a quick nod.

"We're just finishing up sorting through the ingredients for Grandpapa's jam. Wanna help?" asked Tooan. His smile was warm and inviting.

"Umm, actually, I'm supposed to talk with my best friend on WhatsApp. So…maybe next time?" Saira replied, beelining for the door, the wooden bowl still nestled up against her side.

Once in the bedroom, Saira slammed the door shut. "Nak, something crazy has happened…" she whispered. "I think… I think the spirits are alive!"

"Chica, what's going on? Talk!"

Saira spent the next few minutes rambling off all the details she could remember about going out for a walk with 'Wat'si, waking up under the tent, meeting Wamta, the potlatch, the Wild Woman of the Woods, the plank houses and then her finally back to Grandpapa's place.

"And so, yah… that's it. That's the story. Crazy isn't it?" she finished, catching her breath. "So? Whad'ya think? How did I get there? It must have been the spirits, right? But why? Why did they send me back in time? Why to *this* place?" There was a long pause at the other end of the phone. "Nak? Nak, you still there?"

"Yah," answered Nakawe. "Si, I heard you. Are you sure though, Saira? I mean, maybe… this girl Wamta, like, she could have been playing a trick on you, yah know? I mean, sorry, but this all sounds, like, kinda ridiculous…"

"I know, Nak, I know. But I'm telling you, it *was* real. I don't even have my shoes anymore. I left them there – you know, in the past world. And I even have the bowl that Wamta gave me. It's in my hands right now!"

"Woah. Ok," said Nakawe. "I mean maybe — *maybe* – it's possible that you entered into an ania of some sort."

"A what?"

"Ania. Remember when you and your mom joined the Easter ritual in my grandparents' village?"

"Yah. That was totally weird," said Saira. "Different dream worlds or something? Places like the enchanted world and spirit worlds that we can move through?"

"Si, exactly. I don't know for sure, but maybe… this magic stone allows you to travel into past aniam…."

Another long pause.

"If — and I mean only *if* — this is the case, you are so lucky, chica. This is pretty unbelievable. But, also, totally cool!"

For a moment Saira almost felt bad for having this adventure without Nakawe. But what could she do? She had to share her story with someone…

"So, do you think I should tell Grandpapa? Or anyone? Should I try to go back? I'm totally curious about Wamta's brother… I mean, who knows, maybe I can help her with that?"

"Let me think," said Nakawe. "You should be careful. I don't think anyone should know about your magic stone's powers, if it is true. Also, take some pics when you go back, because you will go back, right? I bet you've been transported back there because the spirits think you can help. The natural world is like that… fixing past mistakes and stuff. Oh, and take a picture of that bowl — that teacup thing — you brought back with you. I want to see it."

After the girls hung up, Saira snapped a photo of the wooden bowl and sent it off to Nakawe. She stared at the bowl for a few minutes. She hadn't really examined it closely until now. The design was quite beautiful — it was some kind of creature with two faces, one on top of the other. The one on top had a flat nose, large slanted eyes and red lips with a tongue. The tongue was extending into another creature. The second design was harder to see.

Just then, Saira heard the familiar rumble of Grandpapa's car driving up. She wrapped the bowl up in a loose pillowcase and placed it at the back of the closet before heading down the stairs.

The rest of the day Saira sat outside on the porch swing, reading through her book *Great Animal Spirits of the Pacific Northwest*. She was anxious to go back to the office to get some more tobacco for her stone, but she knew Grandpapa and Tooan were in there. Every few minutes, she'd take the magic stone out and rub it round in her fingers.

"Are you there? Are you still in there?" she said under her breath. But she felt nothing and saw nothing. She went back to reading. Then something pinched at her bum. She jumped up and looked down at the swing. *Was that an insect? Was there a loose wood splinter somewhere?* She rubbed her fingers carefully over the cedar boards. They were all perfectly smooth and there didn't seem to be any sign of a bug anywhere. She sat back down. Sure enough, a couple seconds later, she felt the same little pinch. *What the –?* she thought, leaping up once more. Then she heard a small giggle.

I must be going crazy! It just sounded like the swing just laughed at me! Saira got down on her knees to examine the wooden swing. But still, there was nothing suspicious. Letting out a deep sigh, she grabbed one of the cushions and stretched out across the porch to continued reading.

Grandpapa's book was really interesting. There was so much to learn about First Nations' beliefs in spirits and the animist world. They had songs, dances, stories and even special objects, like wooden teabowls, that were about honouring animal, plant and human spirits. In their culture, the natural world was very powerful. They believed they were related to specific beings, like the salmon, raven or even a cedar tree. Saira was also learning about how different clans and families developed their own crests. These symbols represented their animal or supernatural ancestors. This fascinated Saira. She didn't know much about her own family, really. Aside from Grandpapa, Saira never met any of her other grandparents, on either side. This made her sad, especially when she saw Nakawe's family. They had four generations living all under the same roof! Saira liked the idea of belonging to a long line of people and having an animal symbol represent this family over centuries.

I wonder what animal crest we'd be, she thought, staring up into the sky. *Maybe an eagle? Or an orca whale? Or maybe something exotic like a thunderbird?*

She continued flipping through her book reading about what the various animals meant. There were sections on spirits who had power and wealth and a final chapter on supernatural women. In the last chapter, Saira found a picture that looked exactly like the Wild Woman of the Woods. The drawing had the same wide, bright red eyes and thick lips. According to Grandpapa's book, this creature was also called Tsonoqwa and she was a giant and fearsome forest being who used sweets, food and copper treasures to lure disobedient children into the basket on her back.

"Hey, whatcha reading?" piped up Satsam, appearing on the porch. He was peering over Saira's shoulder.

"Geesus! You scared me!" yelped Saira, nearly dropping the book. "What? This? It's a book Grandpapa wrote," she said, showing Satsam the cover. "It's all about animal spirits and how —"

"I know that book," interrupted Satsam. "My dad wrote it."

"Umm, noooo, he did not," retorted Saira, turning the book over. "Look — Rinaldo Acosta," she said, tapping her finger across the cover. "Says right here."

"Of course, it is!" sneered Satsam. A smirk was forming at the corners of his mouth. "Your grandpa's the famous one. My dad barely went to school. Well, unless you count residential school. But that was hell…. He's the one who's First Nations – Coast Salish and Kwakwaka'wakw. He taught your grandpa everything in there," he continued, grabbing for the book.

Saira could feel her face burning up. She narrowed her gaze at Satsam. "Yah, right! I don't believe you!" she snapped lunging back for the book.

"Believe what?" said a voice behind her. Grandpapa and Tooan were both standing on the porch behind them. Saira and Satsam jumped with surprise.

"Nothing," they answered in unison.

After Tooan and Satsam went home, Saira waited until Grandpapa started supper before slipping away to his office. She needed to see if there were any more bits of smudge stick left, but she also didn't want Grandpapa to get suspicious.

When she got to his office door, it was locked. *Ugh!* she thought, biting her lip impatiently. Then she remembered the key ring dangling from the wall in the room where she'd met Tooan.

Sure enough, the door at the back of the hall was open. Grandpapa was still coughing in the kitchen, so she had some time. She was also curious what Tooan had been doing in this room.

Saira darted inside. It looked like an explosion of boxes had gone off. Some were open, others were labeled and sealed up with tape. More were scattered around the room, on their sides or upside down. A few were piled up high, one atop the other, like a teetering Jenga set.

Saira scanned the open boxes. One was filled with framed certificates. Saira flipped through them: a doctorate in cultural anthropology, a couple honorary degrees in philosophy and medicine and an elaborate looking certificate of shamanic healing from South America. In another box she found a collection of framed and unframed photos. She quickly sorted through them too. There were a few pictures of Grandpapa when he was younger and much, much skinnier. He was receiving some award on stage. She found another one of him and Grandma overlooking the Comox Bay. She had only ever seen a couple photos of her. She and her mom could have been sisters. Every time her mom talked about the past, she got a strange and faraway look in her eye. Saira never asked anything else.

Suddenly she heard a soft rustling followed by a *"Ssshhwwweee, ssshhwwweee!"*

What? What is that? Where is it coming from? Saira heard the sound coming from a box labeled *Culture and Power*. But when she peeked in, she couldn't find anything other than a few more books.

"Ssshhwwweee, ssshhwwweee!"

Saira moved onto two other boxes – one labelled *Magic and Healing,* the other *Indigenous Art.* Again, Saira found nothing, yet the *ssshhwwweee, ssshhwwweee* continued. It was coming from an open box labelled SORT in large handwriting. Inside Saira found a whole array of random objects – loose bits of paper with notes scribbled across, some tape, a stapler, a large magnify glass, a few random sticks and stones with leather strings and a maroon coloured leather notebook with the outline of a small circular seal that was missing. The *ssshhwwweee, ssshhwwweee* was coming from a tiny spider crawling across the notebook. Saira picked it up by one of its legs and moved it over to the open windowsill where it scampered out.

She went back to the notebook, rubbing her fingers over the faded circle. She opened the cover and flipped through. The first few pages looked like a school workbook. *Is this Grandpapa's?* she wondered. There were some basic multiplication exercises, a few vocabulary lessons and even a section with the names of places scribbled in faded pencil. About half-way through the notebook, the writing switched to pen and at the top of each page were the names of more places around the world: Iquitos, Belize, Cotonou. Under each place were a list of names: Pedro, Malick, Surya and others. Then, next to each name, were another few words, all in a language Saira didn't recognize. There were lots of C, E, H's and apostrophes.

Just then Saira heard Grandpapa calling for dinner. She wouldn't have time to get the tobacco. She returned the notebook to the box and headed back to the kitchen.

———— • ————

Over supper, Saira decided she wanted to learn more about his book. "Grandpapa, do you really believe in the animal spirits and supernatural beings you wrote about in your book?" she asked, looking up from her plate of littleneck and butter clams. Her book was on the chair next to her.

"Good question, kiddo," Grandpapa answered, wiping this mouth with a napkin. Four little white pills sat next to his glass. "What we — non-Indigenous people, I mean — need to understand is that the Indigenous people have a very strong mythology that includes their entire natural environment. You know, the trees, animals, plants, even seasons… they believe everything has a soul. This is called 'animist belief'. But this belief goes further. They also believe these souls are interconnected and we are at one with everything." He paused staring down at Saira through the tip of his spectacles. "Do you understand what *interconnected* means?"

"Yah, I think so," answered Saira. "You mean they, like, depend on each other."

"Exactly. Imagine a spider's web," Grandpapa continued, using the back of his fork to outline an imaginary web on the table. "Now imagine all of us living in this web together. But not only that, this web is built on the values of mutual respect and sharing. An animal is not just something to kill for food or clothes, but also to care for and live with. And the trees, plants and flowers are not only to cut or eat, but to also care for and protect. *Our* survival depends on *their* survival."

"That makes sense. So, Indigenous people like to treat animals and plants as their family, or maybe even their friends?" asked Saira, her chin resting in her hand.

Grandpapa nodded. "That's a very good way of putting it. Indigenous really do see animals as their friends. You know, they used to say that the cedar tree was an Indian's best friend. We don't say 'Indian' anymore. That can be derogatory. But you understand what I mean, right? It's like saying even the cedar tree is part of the same family. That's also why you'll see family crests that are animals. These represent their families' stories in a way."

"Cool," said Saira, twisting her thread bracelet round. "That's why they give animals a human side and why different animals mean different things, like *human*-things?"

"Bingo, kiddo! In different Indigenous cultures, animals help explain different life teachings. They aren't their gods, but they are helpers and guides in a way...You know, the things your mom and dad teach you about being honest and good to one another. But animals are also used in creation stories, like the Queneesh story we talked about last night where the glacier was actually a whale that saved everyone."

"And what about this Wild Woman thing?" asked Saira, tapping the book. "You know the one with all the black fur and those big scary eyes?"

"Oh, you mean Tal?"

Saira bobbed her head enthusiastically. "Yes, I was just at a potla—."

Grandpapa's eyebrows curled up like two fuzzy caterpillars "Oh? You were at a potlatch? When was this?"

"I— I mean...I wasn't *at* one, at one. I just *saw* one... you know, like, on YouTube," sputtered Saira, her cheeks growing flush.

"Hmmm...I see," said Grandpapa, returning to his plate of clams. "Anyway, here on Vancouver Island, and among many Indigenous groups, animals are believed to be transformational. This means they can change from animals into humans and vice-versa. And they have the same human-like personalities and values."

"That's so cool," said Saira, pushing the clams with a fork round on her plate. "I wonder what animal I'd be then?"

Grandpapa chuckled. "Well, my little traveller," he said, scooping up his four pills and tossing them back with a gulp of water. "You can think about that while you're in dream land tonight. Bedtime!"

That night, before crawling into bed, Saira checked her phone. Two missed calls from her mom and a message from Nakawe. She wanted a magic stone update:

Didn't have time 2 find more tobacco. Any other ideas??

Saira looked down at the stone around her neck. Funny how such a simple rock could hold such powers. She still wished the stone could help her with her parents, but she also wanted to travel back to see Wamta again. She took the leather string off, placing it on the bedside table. The leather was so tarnished it looked like it would soon disintegrate. The last thing she wanted was to lose something so precious.

CHAPTER 5

That night Saira dreamed she was a salmon. Round and round she swam in the bay, her iridescent skin glimmering with every flicker of sunlight that bounced off her silvery scales. Her belly was large and white; the top of her body a metallic turquoise. She dove to catch some tiny black insects in her hooked mouth, then retreated back to the top of the water. A surge of energy rushed through her body. She felt strong and free gliding through the cool, clear water.

Out of nowhere, another salmon — slightly larger — playfully swung its tail up against Saira's own fish body. They dove, chasing one another in circles and racing to catch the bits of plankton drifting through the water. As they moved closer to shore, the shadow of a large moving creature flew over top. The two salmon froze. Was it an eagle? Saira could just make out the wings and shaggy feathers along its neck. It was a raven. It was chasing a small frog who was fleeing along the riverbank.

The other salmon dove back under. "Look out!" he cried to Saira.

But it was too late for the frog. The raven was already on its way back up into the sky, one of the frog's legs lodged firmly in its beak. From below, a much smaller bird was speeding after the raven. Saira and the other salmon watched in amazement. It was a hummingbird and it was whirling its wings frantically poking at the raven from behind. But the raven refused the distraction. With his talons, he grabbed for the hummingbird and soared up into a nearby cedar tree carrying both the frog and hummingbird firmly in his grasp.

When Saira woke, her head was spinning. She felt a sadness in her belly. *Wow! These animal spirits are really getting to me!* she thought, rubbing her forehead. The dream was so similar to the night before, but this time Saira felt completely helpless. *Was there anything I could have done to save the frog or the hummingbird?*

She grabbed her magic stone. *Maybe I just need a break from Grandpapa's book for a few days? I'll focus on going back to see Wamta,* she thought to herself. *Maybe I really can help find out what happened to her brother? Maybe with my magic stone I can actually do something. Maybe...*

Just then, her phone beeped. It was Nakawe: *My yaya says dead shamans in magic stones r super tricky. They come alive when they meet other spirits. Not sure if helps??*

What does this mean, Saira thought, thinking about what Nakawe's grandmother said. *Other spirits? Where in the world can I find more?*

At breakfast, Grandpapa told Saira that Tooan and Satsam would be coming back shortly. "Just to help work in the garden, move some boxes, you know, that kind of stuff," Grandpapa said casually. "Better for you anyway, kiddo. You'll have someone more your age to hang out with," he continued, sprinkling dried salal berries over two bowls of yoghurt and granola.

"Right," responded Saira. She found Satsam annoying, more than anything. Like one of those noisy wasps buzzing around her breakfast plate in the mornings. But like it or not, Saira knew that if her magic stone didn't start to work again soon, she'd be getting pretty bored.

Grandpapa passed Saira a bowl of cereal. "Your mom was trying to get ahold of you yesterday," he said, pouring some dandelion tea into a mug. "I'm looking to sell the house, the entire property really. I'm getting on in years and it's becoming too much for me to keep up on my own... even with Tooan's help." He stopped to cough into his elbow, then began stirring his tea. The clanging of the spoon against the sides of the mug was irritating Saira. He took a long, noisy sip. "I'm not feeling like I did in my prime anymore... That's why I've always said, it's good to travel and see the world while you can. There's so much to learn and explore out there. Before you know it, your time's up..." His voice trailed off. His face took on a wistful quality.

Saira soften and began mixing up her bowl of granola. "Where will you go, Grandpapa? Will you stay here? In Comox?"

"If I make it that long, I do! No, just kidding... I think I've seen enough of the world though, and then some... I don't want to move anywhere else. Too many memories here. Your Grandma and I moved into this very house before we had kids, you know. Then she got very sick..."

"Kids?" interrupted Saira, nearly dropping her spoon. "You mean you had more than just my mom?"

"Oh no! Gosh, is that what I said? I really am losing it, aren't I. No, 'kid' — I meant 'kid', as in, your mom. We just had one. That's all. Never had time for another... sad, really."

This was perhaps the only time Saira ever remembered Grandpapa talking about her grandmother and though he seemed a bit uncomfortable, she wanted to learn more. "What was she like, Grandpapa?" asked Saira, putting her spoon down.

"Who? Your Grandmother?" he asked as if lost in another world. "Petah — your Grandmother — was...well...she was the most amazing person I'd ever met. Always making me see the world differently, challenging me, helping me grow... I'd have done anything for her. And I did! Well, I *tried*, that's for sure. But she left me too soon," he continued. His smile was disappearing and a dark hue fell over his face. "How my life would have been different had she lived…" Their conversation was interrupted by a call from the kitchen.

"Morn!"

It was Tooan and Satsam. Both were dressed in work overalls. Tooan wore his usual broad smile. Satsam looked less than enthusiastic leaning on a shovel with a few gardening tools poking out from a pail. His baseball-cap was on backwards and his thumb looped through his overall belt hoop like a cowboy.

"Hey there!" cried Grandpapa in a sudden burst of energy. "Grab yourselves a cup of tea from the kitchen. Satsam, Saira's going to help you today. Tooan, we'll tend to my office again."

———————

That day Saira worked in the garden with Satsam. He showed her how to pull weeds, prune shrubs and deadhead some of the bedding plants. He seemed to know a lot about gardening. It was a tiresome job and for the most part they hardly spoke. Satsam showed her what to do and where, then he went off to work on another part of the garden. It didn't bother Saira much, anyway. She preferred the time alone to let her mind wander. She kept thinking back to Wamta. There was something so familiar and comforting about this girl. She and her mom both seemed so kind. But she also felt a deep sadness when she spoke of her brother. Saira really wanted to learn more about him.

As she was removing the dead flower heads on some pink and white cosmos, she accidentally tugged on a bumble bee. "Aaah!" she yelped. But the bee didn't sting her. It simply turned its black furry head around and began tickling the palm of her hand with its antenna. Then it squeaked. "Hiya!"

Saira furrowed her brows and peered in closer at the bumblebee. *Wait. What? Did this bee just tickle me and say hello?*

The bee smiled back, then winked. Before Saira could react, she heard a voice pipe up behind her.

"Hey! Whatcha looking at there?" It was Tooan. He was coming by carrying two tall glasses of iced dandelion tea.

"Nothing," said Saira quickly. The bee buzzed away.

"Here, have something to drink. It's lunch time," he said, waving Satsam over. The three of them walked back to the porch.

'Wat'si laid curled up in a ball under the table. Grandpapa wanted to continue working in the office, so he and Tooan took their sandwiches inside leaving Satsam and Saira to eat alone.

"What's your story?" asked Satsam, taking an enormous bite out of his chicken salad sandwich. It was the only real question he'd asked her since they'd met.

"My — ah — *story?*" repeated Saira.

"Yah, like *who* are you? Where'd you come from? Where are you going?" Satsam continued with a laugh. "You know, those kinds of things."

"Oh! Umm…" Saira started to stammer. She wasn't used to someone being so direct, let alone bombarding her with personal questions. And quite honestly, she didn't really know how to answer them. "I've come here from Montreal. My mom — she is… well, she's Grandpapa's daughter and, my home, I guess I don't really know my home anymore. I'm kinda from everywhere," she continued, clearing her throat. "I was born in Syria, but then we moved to Kenya, then to Mexico, then to Canada. But now, my parents are getting divorced. And that's why I'm here. So, after this happens, I don't know where I'll be… I'm an only child and, I guess we have no family other than Grandpapa. So maybe I'll just be with my mom. That means home is anywhere, really," she finished, looking down at her plate and swallowing hard. She felt exhausted.

"Hmmm," Satsam replied, chewing up the last bites of his sandwich. "Sounds like you're still figuring it all out then…That's cool. You're a bit like me then. I've got no family either, other than my dad that is…I've met your mom though," he continued, taking a huge gulp of his iced tea. "Cool lady. I think she and my dad go way back, but man does she have a chip on her shoulder about your Grandpapa!"

"What are you talking about?!" said Saira. She was finding Satsam's comments rude. First, he said Grandpapa didn't write his own book and now he says he and her mom didn't get along. "My mom has never even *mentioned* you or your dad before. And, she has no chip anywhere," she hissed.

Satsam grabbed his plate and headed back into the house. "Whatever."

Over the next few days, Saira and Satsam continued working together in the garden. Mostly they worked in silence, though on their iced tea breaks they did talk about many things. Saira put her magic rock in the medicine pouch and started carrying it in the zipper pocket of her cargo pants for safekeeping. She also didn't want Satsam to see it. Saira learned that Satsam was Cherokee on his mother's side and that his name actually meant 'Spring salmon'.

"They say I was born on a 'fine April day when the fish were jumping'," he explained. "My family is matrilineal. Even my dad changed his name to a Cherokee one before my mom passed. His name, Tooan-tuh, means frog."

Satsam also showed Saira a few things he learned from his Dad, like traditional wood carving techniques. "You gotta move the blade through the wood like this," he said, paring the knife up and away from his face with quick, sturdy movements. He was showing Saira on a small cedar tree branch. "Chips can fly up into your face if you're not careful. That's what happened to my Dad," he said, tapping his fingers over his eyebrow. "The cool thing about carving is that the spirit already lives in the wood. The carver is just allowing the spirit to take shape."

As Satsam was cutting through the wood, Saira was sure she heard faint sounds coming from the wood chips. *Eeeyyaaa, eeeyyaaa!* She shook her head from side to side.

"You OK there?" asked Satsam, smiling up at Saira.

"Yah, yah, fine." Saira narrowed her gaze at the cedar tree branch. The sound stopped.

Satsam also showed Saira how to identify edible plants, in case she ever got lost in the woods. There were so many different foods to eat in Grandpapa's backyard. Satsam pointed out salmonberries, salal berries, huckleberries, nettle, blue camas, dandelions, arrowhead, milkcaps and cow parsnips. He also showed her the highly poisonous ones like foxglove, hemlock and American pokeweed.

His eyes were twinkling. "If you eat enough, it'll kill you!" he said, pointing out the beautiful pink and yellow coloured flowers.

One afternoon, when Saira was alone looking through the wild flowers next to Grandpapa's garden shed, she swore she could hear light laughter coming from the lily of the valleys. When she leaned down to listen, the laughter stopped. Then as soon as she stood up again, it resumed.

It's true. I am going crazy, she said to herself shaking her head. *Learning about all this nature is causing me to imagine things!*

Though Saira loved learning new things from Satsam, she couldn't stop thinking about her magic stone. It had been several days and she still wasn't able to get her hands on any smudge or tobacco. She was only staying at Grandpapa's another week and was growing impatient. Whenever she knew Satsam wasn't around, she'd whip out the small black rock from the medicine pouch. "Are you in there?" she'd lean in to whisper. "Take me back to see Wamta!"

Saira was starting to think she might have actually imagined the entire episode. It was hard enough to convince Nakawe that her experience was real, and now she was starting to doubt herself, especially now that she was hearing things from plants and insects. But Nakawe was still interested in the idea of a magic stone. She told Saira she'd search on her own side about the types of spirits that might exist and how the magic might eventually return.

"Whatever you do – *if* you do go back – you must take photos," Nakawe pleaded. "I mean, I pretty much believe you, but it's just better... better *proof* you know, if you have pics..."

Finally, one late afternoon, Saira worked up the courage to ask Satsam. "Do you believe in magic spirits or supernatural beings," she asked, pretending to be examining the end of a cedar tree needle.

"Course!" answered Satsam, as if it were the most natural question in the world. A few seconds later he asked, "Why?"

"No reason, really. Just curious..."

"No way! No one just asks a question like that out of nowhere," said Satsam, dropping his hand shovel. "Did you see or hear something? There are spirits and supernatural creatures everywhere you know," he said, looking around.

"Do you know about Tal?" asked Saira.

Satsam stuck out his bottom lip and nodded. "Impressive. Not many people call her by that name. How do you know about her?"

"Oh, the book, that's all..." replied Saira, breaking his gaze. "So, have you ever met her or anything?"

"No, I haven't seen her personally. But she's out there, that's for sure. At night, when you hear the wind blowing through the cedar trees, that's her. That's why you'll never find me going out on a windy day, 'specially at night. No way, man. I don't want to be picked up by some cannibal giant!"

"Yah, good to know," said Saira her voice tinged with sarcasm. "Anyway, I'm tired of gardening, and it's not windy. I'm going to pick some more dandelions. For Grandpapa's tea."

And before Satsam could reply, she tossed her gloves, grabbed a pail and headed down towards the bay. Approaching the water, Saira noticed a conspiracy of ravens circling overhead. Directly below them was the very stump where 'Wat'si had chased the snake a few days earlier and where she'd heard the weird sounds when she'd returned from meeting Wamta. She knelt down to pluck a few large dandelions that were growing alongside the salmonberry bush. But it wasn't just an old cedar tree she was looking at. It was the remains of what looked to be a totem pole. The base was about a metre in diametre and it looked like it had been jaggedly cut with an axe. She could just make out the faded colouring of red and green paint inside the indents of a carved ovoid at the bottom. She placed her hand on the stump and ran her index finger along the wood. As soon as her skin touched the splinters of cedar her entire body began to shake. It started with her toes, then moved up to her calves, through her thighs and jolted into her belly. By the time it reached her head, her eyes rolled up and back, her arms froze and all around her, the world caved in.

CHAPTER 6

When Saira woke, her hands were clutched around the base of the stump and she was staring directly back at a big red tongue. The tongue was part of a wide green face with red lips and bulging black eyes.

Saira tilted her head way back to get a better perspective. The stump was actually a totem pole and it was towering at least 20 metres above her. She arched her neck even further to see the top. She could barely make out the remaining designs as her gaze inched its way up. It looked like there were two fish touching the green creature's tongue. One fish's body was purple, the other turquoise. Between their tails was some kind of bird with a long needle-like beak and wings that spread around the pole. At the very top there was another bird, but Saira couldn't see what it was. Large horizontal wings carved of wood stretched out on both sides. She was sure this was the same pole she'd arrived at the last time she was here. It must have been unveiled after the potlatch ceremony. It was now standing in front of the small entrance leading to Wamta's family's house.

I did it! Saira was filled with excitement and disbelief. She gave her medicine pouch a quick squeeze through her pant pocket. *Thank you, spirits! I was starting to give up on you...*

Just then, the door to the house flung open and Wamta tore out carrying a large cedar bark basket. She nearly walked straight into Saira. "You came back! What happened? I didn't hear from you...you just disappeared... and you took my brother's bowl!" she continued.

"I'm so sorry, Wamta. Really. I wanted to come back earlier," Saira started, "but I…I was having some trouble getting here, let's just say."

Wamta looked confused. "You left in a puff of smoke. It was really weird."

Saira had no idea how to explain what was happening. "I'm just sorry. Really. I had to go," she finally replied.

Wamta edged Saira to the side. "I think it's best if we don't speak here," she hushed. "Already people were asking after seeing you at our potlatch. Some even saw that funny-looking thing in your hands. Let's go somewhere to talk. Wanna come with me to get some berries?"

"Sure. Like, in town? The grocery store?"

"The *what*? We're not going to any store! No, we get our berries here, outside," Wamta said, pointing towards the forest. "Take this basket, I'll show you. We'll get some berries, mint and basil for our jam," she continued.

When they were far enough from sight, Wamta put her hand out signaling Saira to stop. She closed her eyes, took a deep breath in, then got down on her knees. All around them were cedar, fir, spruce and pine trees shooting up into the sky like natural skyscrapers. The smell was intoxicating. Wamta bent down, touching her head to the ground. She was practically kissing the earth. Saira couldn't hear what she was saying. It looked like she might be praying.

Wamta lifted her head. "I'm giving thanks to the Long-Life Maker and our Creator." She picked up a pinch of soil, rubbing it slowly between her fingers. "We are thankful for whatever nature has to offer." She saw Saira's puzzled expression. "We must move through nature with respect, careful to take only what we need and leave some berries for the animals."

Saira smiled. She liked the idea of being grateful for what the plants and trees gave them. When she opened her eyes, she realized they were actually very close to where Grandpapa's house would soon be built. How strange it was without any gates or driveways. No sound of lawnmowers or cars, dogs being walked or cars driving by. Just the chirping of birds and the soft, howling wind.

The girls continued into the forest. They found some huckleberry bushes and began picking them one by one, careful not to disturb the surrounding shrub. As they veered off the path, venturing deeper into the trees, Wamta stopped beneath an enormous cedar tree. "And now, I present to you my best friend," she announced, a large grin spread across her lips. Her hands were caressing the trunk's wide base.

"Did you know we have more than 40 words in Kwak'wala for the Western Red Cedar?" she asked without waiting for a response. "We make everything from this tree... canoes, masks, homes, clothes, even food."

"Wow," said Saira, looking up at the long drooping branches. The afternoon sun was casting sparkles of light along the tips of the tree and she could hear the loud cries of ravens circling overhead.

"I also call it my 'Truth Tree'," said Wamta. "I tell it secrets because I know its spirit will protect me."

There was a long pause. Saira placed her own hands on the tree trunk, next to her friend's. "Hey. Talking about secrets... I really need you to believe something."

"What's that?" Wamta asked. She was still pressing her hand against the bark.

"I actually *do* come from the future. Honestly. From the year 2020 to be exact. I know, this sounds crazy. And it *is* crazy, but I got this magic rock and it seems to allow me to time travel," Saira continued. "I think there is some connection with the kikw, the totem pole. There *must* be. Both times that I've touched the pole in the future, I get transported back to the present."

Wamta took her hands off the tree and looked Saira straight on. "You're really serious about this, aren't you?" she said. For several seconds she said nothing. "I do believe in the spirit world. It's in my culture, so of course I do," she began, "but time travel...I'm not sure...If you really do come from the future, then why? Why are you here?"

Saira just shook her head. "I-I just don't know...Maybe I'm supposed to help you?" she started. "I mean, maybe, *maybe* I can help with your missing brother. Or, maybe that's just stupid. I don't know..." There was an uncomfortable silence.

"If you really *do* come from the future, maybe you can find my brother over there?" Wamta said, pointing her finger ahead. "I mean, in the future he'd be very old now, I guess... maybe eighty or something."

Saira was thinking about someone Grandpapa's age.

"I've never told anyone this," Wamta said, as she took a seat under the cedar tree. She started playing with the fronds of a nearby fern. "The last time I was with my brother we were walking right here," she continued, motioning towards the path. "We went out to pick berries, just like we are today." Wamta paused, blinking hard. "We were *so* competitive with each other," she said, forcing a laugh. "Who could pick the most berries? That was our game. It was usually him, that's for sure. But this time I had spotted a secret blackberry patch, so I snuck off to get them when his back was turned. The most dangerous things we have here are bears or cougars — but they stay out of our way — and then there's Tal... though I'm not sure if I really believe in her." Wamta noticed the perplexed look on Saira's face.

"Remember? Tal? Our Wild Woman of the Woods?"

Saira smiled and took a seat next to Wamta.

"That was the last time I saw my brother. He disappeared that day. Everyone said she took him. I just don't know... She takes children who are naughty. He wasn't either. In any way. The opposite, really. You know the 'good one' — always listening to our abas and ump — that's our mother and father. Even at the residential school, which he hated, his report cards were perfect A's. When he came home, he wanted me to teach him our language and songs. He forgot nearly all his culture. Can you imagine that?" Wamta said, her eyes wide. "That's incredible, isn't it? They drilled it out of him at school. He used to know even more about our culture than me! But after he started at residential school he couldn't even talk to our parents when he came home in the summers. But he was, or maybe still *is,* a very reliable and thoughtful person. He'd do anything for his family and his community. I know he was trying to learn how to write Kwak'wala and Coast Salish. One of the elders was teaching him in secret. I don't know how far he got. But I do know he had beautiful handwriting. One of the nuns taught him calligraphy. I only wish I could write as beautifully as he could."

"How old was he when he left?" Saira asked.

"A year and a half older than me, so, I guess that would make him around 13 at the time. There was no trace of him when he left... well, *nearly* no trace..."

"What do you mean?"

"I did find these really big footprints along a muddy part of the path, next to his basket of berries. They did actually look like feet that could be the size of Tal. They were huge! And where his berries had spilled over, I found a very small piece of fabric stuck to the sharp end of a broken branch. It's not a type of fabric I've seen before. I've kept it in my Bentwood box."

"Can you show me?" asked Saira.

"Sure, why not? Let's get the rest of the berries then we can head home."

The two girls continued down the forested path picking berries along the way. Saira was thinking about Tal and Wamta's brother. She felt like there was more to this story. People don't just disappear. Was Wamta really telling her everything?

After nearly an hour of berry picking, the girls arrived at a small clearing about the size of baseball diamond. Off to the far side of the field was a simple dome-shaped hut sitting low to the ground. It was light-brown and covered in tightly bound bear hide. Bent saplings formed the dome's skeleton and a corner of the door, made of large flowing cloth, flapped gently in the breeze. Outside the door, to the right, was a carved wooden bench. A cedar bark mat laid neatly spread out on the ground next to it.

Wamta stopped at the edge of the trees. She stood perfectly still, then placed her hand up to silence Saira. After a moment, she smiled, then gestured in the direction of the dome. "Do you know what this is?" she whispered.

"It looks like a tent to me."

"It's actually a sweat lodge," Wamta said, swiveling her head back round to make sure no one else was around. "Do you know what that is?"

Saira shook her head.

"A place of purification."

Saira's pupils grew big. "Ooooh."

"Want to see it?"

"Yes. Can we?"

Wamta began to inch forward.

"Was it used recently?" Saira asked, eyeing the remnants of fresh ash sitting in the fire pit.

"Yep, there's a sweat just about every month. I think they had one after our potlatch a few days ago. We call this our *sacred* fire pit," she said pointing to the circle of rocks around the ashes.

The girls continued forward. Saira could feel an electric energy building under her skin. It was making her heart beat faster and the hairs at the back of her neck stand on end. She could tell Wamta was also feeling tense.

"Hell-o?" squeaked Wamta.

Silence.

She signaled for Saira to come closer. She then pulled back the flap on the cloth door and peered in. The girls ducked inside. It was completely dark and the air felt cool and moist. It smelled of herbs and wet soil. The only sound was the throbbing of Saira's heart against her chest.

"Are you OK?" whispered Wamta, reaching for Saira's hand.

"Yah. Totally. I'm fine. It's actually kinda exciting...Can you explain all this?"

"You can't really see it, but there's actually another fire pit in the middle here too," Wamta said. "This is where the fire keeper places seven rocks. They are covered with sacred herbs, like cedar, sweetgrass and tobacco. We call these *offerings*."

Wamta pulled Saira's hand forward so they could make out the darker outline of the rocks. Suddenly a couple of the rocks started to glow a fiery red and orange. Then one seemed to hop like a frog.

"Woah!" Saira cried, jumping back.

"What's wrong?" asked Wamta grabbing for Saira's arm.

"Didn't you —?"

"Didn't I *what?*"

"Oh, never mind," answered Saira, seeing the glowing rocks fade back to black. "I must be — I'm just imaging things."

Wamta took Saira's hand again. "As I was saying, the fire keeper watches over the sweat lodge. It's usually one of our elders, but sometimes it can be I'kinuxw. That's our shaman. Do you know about Spirit Doctors?" Wamta said, looking over at Saira.

Saira was fixated on the rocks.

"Saira? Did you hear me?"

"Sorry, what? Spirit doctors? Yes, I know them," Saira whispered. It wasn't the first time she'd heard of shamans. When she and her mom lived in Mexico, Saira and Nakawe once spied on a shamanic healing session that her mother was doing. She'd never forget the look on her face when she returned from the shaman's tent. It was like her mind had left her body and travelled somewhere far, far away. It was the first time Saira realized that her mom might have another side to her — a side that she'd never know anything about.

"The fire keeper pours special medicinal water over the stones," continued Wamta, walking around the fire pit, one foot in front of the other, as she pretended to pour water from an invisible ladle. "And outside, on the wooden bench, that's where another leader sits to help people who are coming in and out of the sweat. They make sure they're OK – that they don't faint and stuff."

"Nice. It must heat up pretty hot then? How long do you spend in here?" Saira asked.

"Depends. Some people spend hours…I've never been actually. It's only the men who get to go."

"Wow, that's too bad," said Saira thinking about how much she'd hate not being allowed to do something just because she was a girl.

After a few more minutes in the dome, Saira was starting to feel a bit strange. Her heart was no longer beating as fast, but she was feeling dizzy and nauseous. There was a strange vibe, and the glowing rocks were making her feel like she was hallucinating. There was also this uneasy sense that someone — or *something*— was inside the sweat lodge with them. Saira pulled Wamta's arm towards the door. She liked the idea of a purification ceremony, but there was something about the hut that frightened her.

"You're pretty quiet back there," said Wamta shooting her a quick glance as they walked back through the forest. "Everything OK?"

"Totally. I'm fine," said Saira, turning her head back round to see if anyone was following them. Suddenly she stopped dead in her tracks. "Oh my god! Wamta, wait!"

"What?" Wamta asked, spinning around.

"My rock! It can't be! There's a hole in my pocket," she cried, her body paralyzed. She pulled out the inside of her pocket staring at the torn fabric. "It's gone! I need to find it! If I don't… I — I may never get home again!"

CHAPTER 7

For the next hour and a half, the girls retraced their steps. Their eyes darted back and forth across the trail like rapid fire ping pong balls. They scoured the ground for any sign of the missing magic rock, medicine pouch or leather string. They found nothing.

Saira was feeling very uneasy during their search. She swore there were dark shadows following them, but every time she looked around there was nothing but trees and sky, the far-off sound of birds chirping in the forest and a few leaves rustling in the wind. When she lifted her head, all she saw was a lone bald eagle casually circling overhead.

Wamta put her arm around Saira. "I think we should go home and rest. Maybe get a drink and try again later."

Saira had grown quiet. She kept thinking about what would happen if she could never return to the present. She didn't even have her phone with her. She'd never be able to see another photo of her parents or even Nakawe, let alone talk to them. Her stomach felt like it weighed a ton of bricks.

When they entered the plank house, Wamta's mom was there with her baby sister. She was watching her baby closely, rubbing her forehead up and down with her thumb. When she saw the girls arrive, she looked up. "Gilakas'la," she said to both, her lips parting into her warm smile.

Saira's voice was meek. "Gilakas'la," she echoed. "Is your mom OK?" she whispered, leaning towards Wamta.

"Yes, she's fine now, but my little sister was quite ill recently. We think she ate something poisonous, but she seems to be recovering."

Wamta paused for a moment as if uncertain whether to explain more. "My mom believes my sister is the reincarnation of my brother. She was born shortly after he disappeared. So, obviously, she is extra special for her. She calls us all K'walayu, but in the case of my sister I think she means it even more."

"Kwa'layu?" Saira repeated. "What does this mean?"

"The only way I can describe it is something like 'you are the reason for every breath I take'," explained Wamta.

"That's so beautiful," said Saira, thinking about her own mom.

Wamta's mom carried her baby over to another woman on the other side of the house.

Saira looked over. "Wamta, what if my rock fell off in the sweat lodge and it accidentally gets thrown into the fire pit?"

Wamta bit her lip a couple times, then took a deep breath in.

"I have an idea…We can go see I'kinuxw. He's the one who organizes the sweat lodges. He lives a few minutes' walk from here. He has supernatural powers. He might be able to help?"

"Ok," answered Saira, her voice rising. "I've got nothing to lose…literally!" After a moment's reflection, she continued: "Hey, if this I'kinuxw-guy has supernatural powers did you see him about your brother too?"

"Shhh!" hushed Wamta, glancing back at her mom. "We're not allowed to interfere with the spirit world. It's disrespectful. Like I told you, people think Tal took him. This means we need to wait for *her* to return *him*… *if* she does at all."

"Oh, wow. That seems crazy, but fine. Let's head off then."

"Head off?"

"I mean, let's go see this guy about my magic stone."

"Wait. That gives me an idea," said Wamta. "Maybe I can bring the one clue I have about my brother's disappearance. You know, the thing I told you about earlier… I won't show it to him, but maybe he'll sense something if I just carry it with me?"

Wamta looked across the room to check that her mother was still talking. Then she reached over to a large spruce box in the corner and pulled it towards Saira. "This is a bentwood box. My brother made it for me a few months before he disappeared."

The box was beautiful. It was painted in black, white and red and had three rounded corners, a pegged fourth corner and a bottom plank that seemed to be glued on. One side had a shallow relief carving of a hummingbird. It had a long needle nose filled with metal and two pink abalone shells for eyes.

Saira watched as Wamta rustled through bits of cloth, animal skin, books and random wooden carvings. She finally pulled out another box that fit perfectly into the palm of her hands. It had a minuscule salmon head painted on the lid. She then took out a small piece of colourful striped woven fabric. It was no bigger than a small match box and its edges heavily frayed. "I call both of these my 'Wakes' k'awat'si. K'awat'si means box and Wakes was my brother's name. He carved both. See how talented he was? He was really good at freeing the animal spirits from the wood."

Saira smiled.

"This is the only clue I have," said Wamta. She was about to pass the tiny bit of cloth to Saira, just as Wamta's mother looked over.

"Kwa'layu, naxwax'id."

Wamta snapped her fist closed, placing the fabric back in the box before Saira could even touch it. "Coming abas," she replied, leaving Saira to stare at the only piece of evidence of her brother's disappearance now stored back inside the bentwood box.

Wamta's mother asked them to collect sea asparagus for salad and kelp to make donuts. It was the perfect excuse to go visit the I'kinuxw.

Once outside the plank house, Wamta led the way up another long and narrow forested pathway. She was zipping along, the cedar bark baskets bobbing up and down on her arms like flapping bird wings. She didn't want anyone to see them coming this way and they didn't have much time to waste if they had to also collect food for lunch.

After about 20 minutes of walking, the girls approached a small hill covered in moss with long bits of grass flowing in the breeze. A massive cedar tree stood to the right and a tiny cabin-like building attached to the side of the tree. It was like a hobbit's house. The door was made of worn animal skin that lightly dusted the ground. If Wamta hadn't signaled for them to stop, Saira would have walked right on by.

"Wait," she hushed. "He'll know when we're here."

Saira held her breath and started to count in her head to calm her nerves. By the time she reached seven, an odd smell started tickling her nose hairs. It was a pungent scent of dried fish that was sending waves of nausea through her stomach. This was followed by another overpowering feeling; a sense of warmth flooding across her entire body. It started at the crown of her head and trickled downwards like millions of tiny electric shocks zigzagging across her torso. When she opened her eyes, she gasped. There before them, about two metres away, was the oldest man she had ever seen. He stood about five feet tall, his face as wrinkly and rough as cedar bark. He was wearing an oversized tunic made of animal skin that enveloped his tiny frame. His black hair was long and straggly and seemed to merge with his mangled beard at the crux of his chin. In one hand, he held a wooden walking cane, the handle covered in worn leather. His long, wrinkly fingers curled overtop the handle like limp carrots and trembled ever so slightly. He gazed intently at the two girls even though one of his lids dipped down over his left eye. Around his neck, was a thick cedar bark neckring and a couple of necklaces made of claws, bone, stone and wood dangled down across his chest. Wrapped around his forehead was a bandana made of squiggly cedar bark with a few eagle feathers splaying up into the air like shooting arrows.

For a few seconds, the girls and I'kinuxw stood staring at each other in silence. Wamta placed her right hand over her heart and slightly bowed her head. Saira did the same. I'kinuxw remained perfectly still, his gaze transfixed. Then suddenly, without warning, he opened his mouth very slowly and took a deep breath in.

"Gwagwasa'aka," he said, his voice gruff. He spun back round on his bare heels and hobbled back towards his hut with his cane.

Saira looked at Wamta. Her pupils were humungous.

Once inside, I'kinuxw gestured for them to sit. The girls sat cross-legged on a cedar bark mat, while I'kinuxw positioned himself on a deeply worn wooden stump. He began stroking his beard. His stare didn't leave Saira. She wished she wouldn't blush so quickly, but she could feel red splotches warming across her face. She pressed her lips together and looked down. Unsure where to rest her eyes, she then began to search the room.

In the middle of the hut was a fire pit glowing with freshly lit coals. The tiny traces of smoke were dancing their way up a small, chimney-like opening in the roof and off to the side were some barkless sticks of all shapes and sizes. A couple of hand drums were sitting in a corner next to some rolled up animal skins and piles of glass bottles and jars filled with various coloured liquids. On the other side of the hut were some giant walrus tusks and several wooden boxes.

Saira's heart was thumping so fast she thought it might jump straight through her chest. *Could Wamta could hear it?* From the corner of her eye she could see her staring down at her hands, one lay cupped inside the other. *So strange!* Saira thought. *Is she meditating or what?*

I'kinuxw took in another long, slow breath. It made a deep sucking sound. He paused, held his breath, then blew out two loud puffs of air. "The natural world has brought you here," he began, his pupils rolling to the top of his head. "Though you are caught between two worlds." He sharpened his gaze. His look seemed to be staring straight through Saira like she was nothing more than a window into another world. "They have chosen *you*," he said, pointing his long straggly finger at Saira. "Learn the powers of your gift. But stay protected. Remember that magic can be fickle." He paused for several seconds, cleared his throat loudly, then continued. "You may swim between time and place, but secrets serve a purpose that may go untold. Colourful threads of love both protect and reveal."

Both Saira and Wamta looked confused, but they held onto his every word.

I'kinuxw continued: "Spirit beings never die. They transform from animal to man, across time and space. Do not abuse your gift. Responsibilities gone astray turn power away." He then reached behind him and pulled out a small vile of bright purple liquid from under a red cloth. He passed it to Saira, his leathery hand uncurling like a rusty jack-in-the-box. "Should you accept your calling, you will be guided. But you can also never go back," he cautioned.

Saira took the small vile and bowed her head.

"Gilakas'la," said Wamta, placing her hand on Saira's knee. She blinked hard signaling for them to leave.

As the girls left the hut, Saira turned her head back once more to look at I'kinuxw. But instead of an old man, all she saw was a lone bald eagle gazing back.

The girls waited until they were a few minutes away before speaking.

"Ok. So. That. Was. Crazy," said Saira, shaking her head. She was gripping the purple vile tightly in her hand. "All this talk of two worlds, spirits, animals and magic…I mean, come on? Wamta, what does any of this mean? Like, is this for *real*?"

Wamta was lost in thought and still speed-walking through the forest. "What's your spirit animal?" asked Wamta, shooting Saira a quick glance.

"My *what? Spirit* animal? Are you —?"

"We all have one," interrupted Wamta. Her tone was serious. "It's the animal that represents your spirit self."

"Gosh, I have no idea. I've never thought of this before," said Saira. "I guess you know yours?"

"I'm a hummingbird, just like my name, Kwa'akwamta," Wamta said matter-of-factly. "I got it during my Giadas."

"I'm not sure…" Saira started. "Why did they call you this bird? And what's this Gia—?",

"My parents wanted to remind me of my values and qualities. Hummingbirds are supposed to like hard-work, joy, love and healing," she answered. "And you know what else? Hummingbirds are supposed to live in Tal's hair. That's crazy, isn't it?"

"Wow, we-ir-d. And Gia—?" she repeated.

"Giadas," said Wamta. "It's a special ceremony to acquire your power – when a girl turns 12 or so, like I am, you go to a special place with four of our elders, all women too. They give us our powers there and teach us how to keep it.

"So, you – *you* have powers?" asked Saira, pointing her finger at Wamta's chest. "What are they?"

"I'm supposed to bring good health. But, really, that was my brother's gift, not mine."

"What do you mean?"

"Even though his spirit animal was a frog, he had this ability to heal people," explained Wamta. "In the months before he disappeared, he actually worked with I'kinuxw. He'd often be called into the village to help people who were sick."

"Cool," exclaimed Saira. "Your brother was some kind of shaman healer too?"

"We're not positive. But *if* he was, I don't know why he disappeared…I mean if he knows magic and all, he should be powerful enough to come back, right?"

"I don't know, Wamta. But I have no idea about these things. Maybe he didn't want to come back?"

As soon as Saira said that, she realized she shouldn't have. Wamta's tear ducks started to well up.

"Oh, I'm so sorry. My bad. I'm sure he didn't want to leave," Saira said, placing both hands on Wamta's shoulders. "Look, I'm going to ask my friend Nakawe about all this. She's Mexican and knows about these things… Oh, wait. That is *if* I can get back to the present world and talk to her…" Saira said, reminded that she was still without her rock. She looked down at the purple vile.

"It's OK," said Wamta. "We'll find your rock. We have to be positive. And we'll find my brother too," she continued. "Let's *both* be positive."

The girls hugged, then continued on their way. When they were within eyeshot of the village, they headed straight for the water to gather some kelp and sea asparagus. When they got inside the log house Wamta's mom wasn't around. In fact, no one was. There were only a few dogs laying quietly by the fire.

"That's odd. I wonder where everyone is? Well, let me show you what I wanted to show you before," Wamta said, dropping the basket of kelp and sea asparagus by the fire and racing over to her Bentwood box.

She pulled out a colourful piece of torn fabric and passed it over. Saira put down the purple vile from I'kinuxw and reached out to take the small bit of cloth. She rubbed the cotton stripes gently between her fingers eyeing it closely. "Hmm… hard to tell. Funny thing, this reminds me of the traditional fabrics we saw in Mexico," she said, handing the fabric back to Wamta. "If I had my phone with me, I could take a picture of it."

"I doubt it's from Mexico," Wamta replied, placing it back into the Bentwood box. "I mean, how would that even get here? That's miles away!"

"Hey, what's that?" asked Saira, pointing to a small maroon leather notebook in the box. It had an embossed wooden crest on the front.

"This is my brother's school workbook from Port Alberni," said Wamta, pulling it out. "Open it. See how nice his handwriting is…"

Saira extended her hand out to take the notebook. It looked somehow familiar. As soon as she laid her fingers on the cover, she knew what was happening. Small lightning bolts began shooting up her neck and tingling through her skull. Her heart started to beat a mile a minute and her head got very hot. Then, just as suddenly, her whole world froze and everything turned a scorching red, fiery purple, then faded to nothing.

CHAPTER 8

Saira felt groggy. Her neck muscles ached and her stomach felt heavy. She rolled over onto her side and saw the faded red and green outline of an ovoid that was carved into the totem pole's base. A huge feeling of relief washed over her.

Wow, I made it back to the present! To her side, laying amongst the dandelions, was the leather notebook. *But wait. If I'm back in the present, this means I did it without the stone. But — how is that even possible?!*

She reached into her pocket thinking maybe the magic stone was actually still in there. Her stomach dropped. But there was a crinkly piece of paper with a note:

> *Hello Saira,*
>
> *Just in case you make it back to the present world and I don't get the chance to tell you in person. I'm so happy to have met you!*
>
> *Wamta*

Saira held the note for a moment before carefully folding it back into her pocket. She might not have the stone, but she most certainly had a new friend. *Maybe it's the totem pole that's magic,* she thought turning her gaze back to the wooden stump.

From behind, she heard a voice calling.

"Saira! What in the world are you doing? Taking a nap?" said the voice laughing. "Weren't you supposed to be getting dandelions to make some tea?" Satsam was walking towards her waving her phone around high in the air.

"You left your phone at the house, you know. Not a good idea to stray off without it! The Wild Woman of the Woods might get you…ha ha ha!" He was now looking down at her. From this angle, his profile looked so familiar. Saira reached up for her phone.

"Satsam! Are you following me?!" she snapped. "I *am* getting dandelions!" She rolled over onto her belly to hide the notebook. "I was just…just stopping here to look at this totem pole," she said, nodding towards the stump.

"Totem pole, eh?" said Satsam, walking closer. He knelt down beside Saira. "What makes you think it's a —?"

As soon as he saw the ovoid carving, a knowing smile spread across his lips. "Cool, you're right!" he said. "Many of these old poles are still around… My dad says traditionally totem poles, or kikw as he likes to call them, should be left to disintegrate on their own. Kinda like letting nature take back control, I guess…" He reached his hands out to touch the jagged wooden edges.

"No!" cried Saira, grabbing for his hand.

"What the heck?" said Satsam, flinging his hand back as if he were about to touch fire. "What's wrong with you?"

"It's…ah… it's just that you might get a splinter, that's all," said Saira.

"Oh yah, right. I think I can handle a little splinter, Saira…" he answered. And with that, Satsam flung his hand back onto the pole.

———————•———————

Saira let out a scream and pinched her eyelids shut, readying herself for an explosion.

But when she opened them, Satsam had both hands atop the stump and his knees resting against the base. He was whistling away, casually examining all sides of the carving. "Hmm…hmm… hmmmm…"

"Hmmm, what? What are you looking for? Don't you, ah, feel anything strange?"

"Anything *strange*?" repeated Satsam, peering at her from the side. "Like what? A splinter?" he continued with a sneer.

"Yah. A splinter," Saira continued, realizing nothing was going to happen.

"I wonder why my dad has never shown me this one before," mumbled Satsam. "It's on your grandpapa's property, so he must know about it…"

Just then Saira noticed a familiar leather string poking out from around Satsam's neck. "Satsam, what is *that*?" she asked, pointing to his neck.

"What's *what*?"

"That!" she spat, reaching for his neck.

"Hey, back off!" he yelled, leaping up. "This is from my dad," he continued, pulling out the leather string. Sure enough, at the end of the cord, was a twisted black polished stone about five centimetres long. It looked exactly like Saira's magic rock.

"No, it is *not*!" howled Saira. Her face was burning up. "It's mine! Now where did you get that? You must tell me!"

"I told you," continued Satsam. "It's from my dad. Not that it's actually any of your business." He pushed the rock back under his t-shirt and spun around on his heels to head back to Grandpapa's. Saira scrambled to chase after him. "Ha ha, wanna race, do you? Let's go then!"

Satsam was much faster than Saira. He tore along the marshy trail, slaloming through the trees like an Olympic skier. Saira struggled to keep up. She was clutching the leather notebook in her hands. Eventually she had to stop to catch her breath. She was still tired after her long walk with Wamta, but so upset with Satsam.

Once I see Grandpapa, he'll sort it all out, she reassured herself. Pulling out her phone, Saira saw that she'd just missed a call from her mom. It was definitely not the time to talk with her. She first needed to speak with Nakawe. She needed to fill her in on the last couple of days and she needed to get her necklace back, fast.

CHAPTER 9

Back at the house, Grandpapa, Tooan and Satsam were having an early evening drink out on the porch. Saira tucked the notebook under the back of her shirt. Satsam seemed relaxed with his smug look spread clear across his face. He had even pulled the magic rock out from under his T-shirt so it was staring Saira in the face.

"Hey kiddo, Satsam said you went out to get some dandelions for tea?" Grandpapa hollered. His voice cracked, then he broke into a coughing fit. He got up and went inside. Saira suddenly realized she hadn't brought any dandelions back.

"Umm, yah, I was going to...But I...I got distracted," she answered sheepishly.

The amount of time she was away in the past world was actually only a few minutes in the present world, she remembered. This meant it shouldn't be too suspicious if she didn't bring any flowers back. "I'll go back later," she said, taking the porch steps two at a time. She offered a quick hello to Tooan and marched straight past Satsam.

"Grandpapa? Grandpapa?" she pleaded walking into the kitchen. "I need to talk to you about something." He was leaning over the counter, his forehead resting in his hands and swaying back and forth like an injured bird. "Grandpapa? Are you OK?"

"Oh, yes... don't worry, Saira. Just a dizzy spell, that's all," he replied, his voice soft. He lifted his head with effort and forced a weak smile. Grandpapa almost never called Saira by her actual name. His eyes looked even darker, his hair particularly unkept. "Did you talk to your mom today?" he continued, clearing his throat as he reached for his pill canister.

"No, Grandpapa. Not yet. She called, but I missed it. Why? What's up?"

"She's coming out next week."

"She's *what*?" cried Saira. "Is everything OK? Why is she —? I'm going home next week anyway... well, *aren't* I?"

Grandpapa ignored her last question. "Saira, I've asked her to come. I need to see her. It's important. Give her a call...," he continued, taking a swig of water and downing the pills. "Now, what did you want to talk to me about?"

"It's Satsam," Saira started. "He...he stole my magic rock. You know the one from you."

Grandpapa cocked his head to the side.

"You know, the one you gave me when we played global hopscotch?" Saira continued. "The one from Northern Brazil?"

Grandpapa's face remained expressionless.

"The piedra encantada, Grandpapa! I saw it around his neck on the very piece of leather string you gave me!"

"Saira," Grandpapa began slowly, one of his eyelids twitching, "Sorry, but I'm not sure what you're talking about. When we played global hopscotch, you landed on Mexico. I gave you a colourful cotton Yaqui belt. It was from the Sierra Madre mountains. That stone you're referring to — the one around Satsam's neck — it was given to him by his dad, Tooan."

Saira felt like she'd been kicked in the stomach. She excused herself and went directly upstairs. She closed the bedroom door and pulled out her phone to message Nakawe: *Nak, we need 2 talk asap!!! I went back in time, but lost my magic stone. Call me!!!*

She put the leather notebook on her lap and started biting her nails. Less than five minutes later her WhatsApp rang.

"Nak? Hey! Thank goodness. There's so much to tell you. I did it — I went back in time again. With my magic stone, but without any tobacco. So, it must be the stump that did it. It's the second time I've touched the stump — which is actually a totem pole by the way — and when I was in the past, I went berry picking with my new friend Wamta and she showed me a sweat lodge. Do you know what that is? It's so cool, but kinda scary too… I felt a really weird energy in there. Anyway, then when we were walking back to Wamta's house I realized I lost my stone. So, we went to see their shaman, well they call him I'kinuxw. He really gave me the freaks, Nak. And then he gave me some kind of weird purple liquid, which — oh my gosh, I just remembered I think I left it in the past world by accident. But that's not all. I also saw what, might be, a clue about her brother's disappearance. It was a piece of colourful fabric. But then I forgot my phone so I couldn't take any pictures," Saira's voice was racing a mile a minute. "But then, Nak, *then* I got transported back to the present, I'm pretty sure that happened just when I touched this beautiful leather notebook that Wamta showed me — it belonged to her brother. And then — and this is the weirdest part — I arrive back in the present and this guy that I've been working at Grandpapa's house with, the son of his helper I've told you about, well he shows up wearing *my* magic stone around his neck! Can you believe it? And now, he refuses to give it back. So, I tell Grandpapa and he tells me he doesn't know what I'm talking about. That he never gave me a rock. But you know I did, right? I mean, I showed you pictures and we talked about it. Right? Nak? Nakawe? Hey, are you still there?"

There was a long pause at the end of the receiver.

Nakawe finally cleard her throart. "Saira? Are you feeling OK?"

"What are you talking about? I'm fine. A bit tired. But … did you hear what I said?"

"Yes, I did. But I'm confused. I mean, I don't know what you're talking about. This is the first time you're telling me of a magic stone. Don't you mean the colourful sash belt your Grandpapa got from Mexico?"

———◦◦◦———

Saira told Grandpapa that she didn't feel well and needed to go to sleep early. The truth was her head was spinning and she couldn't sleep a wink. Nothing about the day was making sense. She wanted to talk to her mom, but wasn't sure what to say.

"Should you accept your calling, you will be guided. But you can also never go back." she replayed I'kinuxw's words over in her mind. *My calling? What does that mean?* she wondered. *Did this all even really happen?*

Nothing could convince her that Grandpapa had given her a sash instead of a stone when they had played global hopscotch. But why didn't she have any proof? She couldn't understand why both Grandpapa and Nakawe were talking about some colourful sash, when Grandpapa had clearly given her a magic rock! She didn't even know where this sash was, let alone when he might have given it to her. She started flipping back through the photos on her phone, but she couldn't find any pictures of her stone nor any record of texts about the rock with Nakawe. She did find a blurry shot of Wamta at the potlatch though and another of the wooden bowl. She reached up onto the back shelf and pulled the bowl out from inside the pillowcase. As she grabbed the cotton sheet, a colourful cotton belt fell out onto the carpet.

What? Grandpapa's sash! How in the world? She picked up the fabric between her thumb and index finger as if it were a dead bird. *It couldn't be…could it?*

The fabric looked exactly like the piece of cloth she'd seen from Wamta, just a lot more faded. Sure enough, at one end of the sash was a small rip as if a piece of the cloth had snagged off. Saira's heartbeat started to pick up pace. She took out the other three clues from the back of the closet and placed them on her bedspread. There was the wooden bowl, the colourful sash and the leather notebook with the small seal. *What is it with these three things?* she wondered, tapping her bottom lip.

After a minute, she reached for the notebook, running her fingers over the wooden circle. It had an unfamiliar face delicately carved into the seal. There were big pupils, wide lips and a small tongue extending downwards. She undid the knot on the leather string and gave it a sharp tug. The name "Wakes" was written across the inside flap in long, flowy handwriting. She began flipping through the first few pages. It was a school workbook, just like the one she'd seen in the room downstairs. She hadn't noticed if there were dates on that notebook, but this one had dates. The entries started on January 12, 1940. Saira skimmed towards the middle, but strangely the entries stopped. The last date recorded was June 30, 1940. The rest of the notebook was blank.

There's no way this could be the same notebook, she thought to herself. *That would be impossible. Wouldn't it?*

CHAPTER 10

When Saira finally fell asleep that night, she dreamed again that she was a salmon. But this time she was all alone and wasn't swimming peacefully at all. Her belly felt tight and heavy. The night moon was full, sitting high in the sky and the waves from the ocean crashed wildly down all around her. She struggled to push herself through the powerful tide, but she was too weak. In the waves she could see faces — her mom, dad, Nakawe, Grandpapa and a young boy. Her body started to tense up and her breathing was strained. The water all around her was turning a bright amethyst colour, like someone had added a powerful drop of dye. There were long, wooden posts and fishnets made of colourful fabric blocking her in from all sides. She began swimming in circles frantically trying to find an escape. No other fish were around, only the bones of other salmon slowly sailing by.

Saira opened her mouth up wide, taking in a giant gulp of the purple water. She then spotted a small break in the net and broke through. She began swimming towards the shore. As she approached the rocks, she placed her fins up onto their algae-covered surface. A nearby bald eagle stood perched on a rock watching as she struggled to push herself up with one slippery fin and fling herself out of the water. As she propelled herself onto the sand, she looked down in amazement. Her fins had grown into long and narrow spindly legs. Her gaze went back ashore. There before her was a large woman with black fur running into the woods.

"Tal!" she tried to cry, but no sound came out. Just ahead was a hummingbird. It whirled around a cedar tree, buzzing up and down trying to tap nectar from its trunk. It was pecking at the thick bark like a woodpecker.

Saira woke to the sound of a knocking at the door. She checked her phone. It was already past 9am. How did she manage to sleep so long?

"Sleepy head! You OK in there?" Grandpapa almost never came upstairs and his voice sounded hoarser than usual through the bedroom door. "You must be famished, my little traveller? I have some fry bread ready downstairs. I'd also…like to show you something."

Saira quickly stashed the bowl, notebook and sash under her bed before opening the door. Grandpapa was still standing there, his spectacles and cord swaying over the top of his chest, his right elbow leaned up against the wall. The skin on his face looked dark and heavy. It was sagging like stretched, worn out leather. In the palm of his left hand, was a small rock, a thin leather string carefully looped around.

"I think there was a misunderstanding," he started. "You know… about the rock Satsam got from his dad. I thought you might like your own?" He gently pulled the leather around Saira's neck. "This is also from the Amazon. I've got loads."

Saira looked down at the rock hanging off her collarbone. But it wasn't at all the same. This one was circular with brown splotches. She wanted the one she had before. The one with the smooth, glassy surface. The one that resembled a small snake.

"Thanks Grandpapa," was all she said.

———◆———

After breakfast, Grandpapa got a phone call and went out to the garden. Saira took the rock off from around her neck and made a quick break for the room at the back of the hallway. She hadn't been back inside for a few days, but she heard Tooan working in there and knew there must be many more boxes that had been packed up.

Once inside, her eyes darted around the room. She skimmed over a few of the familiar-looking labelled boxes. Finally, she rested on the large box labelled SORT. It was sitting perched on top of a chair, the side flaps wide open. It had clearly been searched through, as there was no leather notebook inside.

Ugh! thought Saira, glancing out the window to check on Grandpapa. She had to work fast if she was to find the notebook.

She whipped her neck back around and immediately rested her gaze on another box. This one was closed and labelled CHECK, also in large sprawling black letters. Inside was the most magnificent wooden face mask Saira had ever seen. It was multi-coloured with big beady white eyes and round black pupils that made it look permanently surprised. It had a small flat nose with large red and green nostrils and big red lips curling up on the sides. Scraggly cedar bark hair fell down around its face. She turned it over to reveal a cross-sectional design, on the inside, carved with small diagonal etchings.

She brought the mask up to her face. It smelled musty, with just a hint of cedar. Saira let her mind travel back to the potlatch where she imagined wearing it as she danced around the warm fire, the comforting smell of wood burning and the sound of batons beating down on the large overturned tree trunk.

"Saira! What are you doing?" It was Tooan standing at the doorway. Satsam was just behind him, a bemused look on his face.

"Oh! You scared me," cried Saira, leaping up from the box. Her face turned the same crimson colour of the mask's lips. "Sorry, I — I was just curious."

"S'ok," Tooan replied, briskly taking the mask from Saira's hands. "You need to be careful though. This is precious. *Very* precious. It's old and with your Grandpapa's move, and all, it's important we keep everything... well, intact."

"Yes. Of course," said Saira readying to leave. "I'll just go see if Grandpapa needs any help now." Saira couldn't get out of the room fast enough. She felt so guilty about looking in these boxes. But then again, it was only a wooden mask she was touching. Wasn't it?

⎯⎯⎯◆⎯⎯⎯

Later that afternoon Saira went outside to talk to her mom. Tooan and Satsam walked by while she was on the phone. They were so deep in conversation that they didn't even notice her. Tooan had a large shovel balanced over one shoulder and Satsam held a few black garbage bags scrunched up under his arm.

"Mmmhmm, yah, fine, Mom," Saira said, gritting her teeth as she caught sight of the magic stone dangling around Satsam's neck. "Nah, not much…He's usually working. Yah, with Tooan, his helper. I guess you know him? That's what his son said…No, I haven't spent much time with either of them. They just walked by… No, I'm mostly just reading the book from you and Dad. Yes, I'm helping Grandpapa. I've been working in the garden…Yah, he told me he'll be moving. He said you're coming out next week, though? How's Dad? Are things OK with you guys again? Yes, ok. Yah, I know you've made your decision. Ok. Fine. Bye."

After she hung up, the divorce knot started to clench in her belly. She'd actually forgotten about it for a few days while she'd been caught up in her time travel experiences, but now, with her magic rock gone, she was probably never going to return to that world. Not only would she never see her new friend again, but she wouldn't be able to help solve the mystery of what happened to her brother. She'd be stuck in the present facing the reality of her parents' break up. There seemed little she could do about it.

Saira's thoughts was interrupted by her phone. It was Nakawe: *Chica! Feeling better? Found this pic of u & ur Mom at the ania Easter ritual at my Grandparents' village. Remember how much fun we had?*

Saira starred at the image. Nakawe had sent her a photo of Saira and her mom dressed up for the festival. She remembered that day like it was yesterday. She had so much fun. They all wore different animal costumes— horses, snakes, wolves, bears and deer — and danced until late in the night under a full moon and stars. Even the kids stayed up late. There was music, food and a few people seemed to actually transform into animals. Their eyes rolled back into their heads as their necks titled way back to the sky. One lady, who wore a silky black robe, got down on all fours and began howling at the moon like a wolf. A couple others galloped around like wild horses, bobbing their heads from side to side, kicking up their legs and arching their backs. Saira was both scared and intrigued. Her mom explained to Saira that it was possible to experience different feelings at the same time, because it was, she believed, possible to live in different places at the same time. She called these "realms of existence" or something like that. For Nakawe, this stuff was normal. It was part of her Yaqui culture. But for Saira, it was, definitely, very new.

Looking down at Nakawe's message something clicked for Saira. *Realms of existence! Living in different worlds at the same time! Maybe she was talking about time travel?* She replied to Nakawe's message: *Thx Nak! I'm fine. Found the sash.* She paused a moment, then sent off another message: *That night was so fun. Have u travelled into aniam b4?*

Nakawe replied almost instantly: *LOL!! In my dreams, chica. Very few peeps can. Heard it's real scary tho!*

The girls continued to message back and forth playing with selfies and sharing new music. The topic of the magic stone and colourful sash never came up. Meanwhile, Grandpapa was in his office, as usual, and Tooan and Satsam were still off doing something outside. At one point, Nakawe had to leave for her grandparents, so the two girls ended their conversation and Saira decided to go out for a walk. She wanted to go down to see the old totem pole stump again.

Approaching the bay, she stopped to watch a bald eagle circling overhead. It was like they were watching over their animal kingdom below, ensuring all was well. Saira had never seen so many eagles before she'd arrived at Grandpapa's.

As she was standing there, she felt a small tug on her pant leg. Looking down, she could see a small butterfly pulling on her cuff. "Hey, what are you doing?" she whispered, inching her hand towards the butterfly. It swiveled its tiny head up towards Saira, smiled, then darted off. *Did that butterfly, really, just smile at me?*

Just then an enormous shadow fell over her. She ducked her head and threw herself forward, trying to avoid whatever it was that seemed to be hurtling above. When she peered up, there was nothing other than a few puffy white clouds in the sky. Even the eagle had disappeared. She looked back down and gasped. A couple feet in front was a huge mound of freshly dug up earth. It was exactly where the totem pole used to be.

CHAPTER 11

Saira dropped to her hands and knees and began digging around.

What in the world? I was just here. How can someone...? Wait. Satsam! He was with his dad earlier... carrying a shovel and bags... But didn't he say totem poles should be left to disintegrate on their own?

Saira stood up and glanced around. There was the giant patch of dandelions and the enormous salmonberry bush. This was definitely were the totem pole had been. She arched her head back up to the sky. The eagle had returned. It was circling round again, its dark brown wings outstretched wide. It started making a high-pitched whistling sound and pulled its neck back. She watched it soar up and down, like a kite bobbing in the wind. Then it pointed its hooked yellow bill downwards as if preparing to dive bomb. But it wasn't her it was targeting. It was the conspiracy of ravens she'd spotted the last time she was there. The eagle sped towards the black birds, sending them fanning out like ripples in the water. It was then that Saira noticed a single white raven among the flock. It was soaring in the air looking straight-on at the eagle in an aerial face off. Saira watched in amazement as the two birds charged one another with their beaks. Eventually, the white raven let out a deep throaty "kraaaa" and relented. It plummeted downwards, sweeping itself just inches above the ground before rebounding upwards again, speeding towards the forest.

Saira watched until the white dot faded from sight. She turned to gaze back up at the sky, but the eagle was gone. She swiveled to her left and saw that it had now perched itself on a large boulder only a few metres away. It was watching Saira with its unnerving yellow eyes. She held her breath. She'd never been so close to a bald eagle, but there was something about its presence that, somehow, seemed comforting. She reached for her phone to take a picture, but then, just as suddenly, the eagle winked before vanishing into a small puff of smoke. Saira stood in disbelief, then crept her way towards the boulder. There, on the rock, exactly where the eagle had stood with its golden talons, was a tiny vile filled with the iridescent purple liquid.

⊷•⊶

Walking back to Grandpapa's, Saira was filled with a nervous energy. She was excited to have witnessed the showdown between the birds and to have seen a white raven again. But she also felt confused about why the stump had been dug up and how she got the vile from I'kinuxw back, which she'd left in the past world. *Could the eagle be trying to communicate with me? But why? And about what?*

Approaching the far gate of Grandpapa's house, she could see that Tooan and Satsam were standing at the back of the yard. They were in the same place she'd seen Tooan digging with the cardboard boxes the morning she'd arrived. It was early evening now, and the sun was slowly making its descent. Saira wanted to be sure they wouldn't see her, so she ducked behind the garden shed. There were large piles of dirt scattered throughout the yard and the black plastic bags she'd seen tucked under Satsam's arm earlier in the day were laying on the ground. Saira squinted to get a better look.

A gruff voice behind her called out. "Spying on them, are you?" It was Grandpapa. He was standing, arms crossed, looking down at her through the bottom of his spectacles.

"Oh!" shrieked Saira, jumping back. "Grandpapa! You scared me! I was...I was just wondering what they were —."

"I know," he interrupted, his hazel eyes flashing. "You were wanting to know what they're doing. Saira, it's OK to be curious. But don't be *too* curious. It can get you into all sorts of trouble."

"I-I...," Saira stammered. Her face grew hot. It wasn't like Grandpapa to be so stern with her. She was feeling very guilty, not only about being caught spying, but being caught doing something that shouldn't be a big deal. Or *should* it? "Sorry, Grandpapa. I'll just head back now," she continued, spinning around towards the house.

She tore up the stairs, the small purple vile jiggling up and down inside her pocket. She swore she'd go back to see what was really going on in the yard. But only after everyone had left.

———◆———

A couple of hours passed before Saira heard Grandpapa's car door slam and his car pull out of the driveway. She peered out through bedroom window. No sign of Tooan or Satsam in the back yard anywhere. *They must have gone home for the day*, she thought. A jittery sensation was rising in her belly. She continued to the hallway window to double-check. Still no sign of anyone. She crept down the stairs, stopping at every step to listen for any sound or sign. Nothing. She continued moving down the stairs and eventually outside to where she'd seen them digging earlier. As she approached the mounds of dirt, she saw that they had separated the plots of dirt with long strings and placed small wooden signs in the soil indicating what had been planted. There was mint, basil, lettuce, tomatoes...But there were no cardboard boxes to be seen anymore. The shovels and bags were also gone. *Weird. Maybe they were really just planting Grandpapa's garden?*

Saira tiptoed between the long mounds of soil. She wasn't much of a gardener, but she did know that planting a vegetable garden in mid-August was late. There was a small sign labelled 'cherry tomatoes' with a long scraggly rope spiraling out from the soil. She gave it a gentle tug, but it wouldn't give. She continued to dig around the rope. The more she dug and brushed away the soil, the more she realized this wasn't just rope. It was actually a piece of cedar bark, just like the hair she'd seen on the Kwakwaka'wakw mask she'd found in the box. She continued digging until her fingers hit something hard. She pushed away the soil and there she saw the multi-coloured mask she found earlier. The very same diagonal etchings were displayed on the inside.

Saira started biting the tip of her thumb as she peered around. *Why did they bury this?* She looked back at the other mounds of soil around her. *Are there other objects buried here?* she thought, laying down her phone and hopping over to the next plot. This one was labelled 'mint and basil'.

Once again, she began lifting through the soil with her hands. She started digging faster and faster. She had no idea when Grandpapa, or even Tooan and Satsam, might come back. Off to the side was a small hand shovel. She began scooping out larger piles of soil, throwing it up into the air like confetti. At one point, the shovel made a clunk. Her heart jumped. She put down the shovel and began plowing through with her hands. Finally, her fingers touched something hard and cold. A familiar tingly sensation followed as it swept through her fingers, hands, arms and then clear up to her head. She felt her brain expanding as if it were about to explode. Stars appeared, then everything went dark.

CHAPTER 12

When Saira woke up, she was laying outside on a cedar bark mat. A large tarp made of animal hide stretched out over top of her. In her hands, Saira held a long wooden shaft attached to a disk-shaped object that held a bundle of thick yarn. It had two concentric circles of different sizes, each carved with images. There was a small hole at its centre. She had no idea what this was, but it looked like some kind of weaving tool.

I made it back! But how did this happen without the magic stone or the stump?

She propped herself up onto her elbows, then slid out from under the tarp. No one else was around, but from behind came the faint sounds of cheering. She squinted in the direction of the water. A large group of people were gathered down on the shore, a bunch of large dugout canoes positioned in the water nearby. Saira put the wooden object down and moved closer, careful to hide behind some nearby fir trees.

The people on shore we wearing short, flat cedar bark hats and carried large hand drums made of deer hide. They were beating against the sides with long sticks and shouting towards the water where a group of six or seven canoes were propelling forward towards the beach. Each boat had elaborately designed sterns that jettied out far beyond the backs of the canoe. The long, tapered bows had cedar branches hanging off the sides. Each canoe held 11 paddlers, including a bow and stern person. They were heaving their bodies back and forth and singing. In rhythm to their chants, they struck the butt end of their black and red paddles against the sides of the canoe.

Saira scanned the crowd for any sign of Wamta. Her eyes rested on a young girl sitting on some rocks, next to a canoe. It was hard to tell from behind, but she had the same long black braid and was wearing a hat. Her calves were dangling over into the water and she seemed to be painting on the boat's stern. The girl lifted her head and turned to the side. Sure enough, it was Wamta.

***

"Psssst," hissed Saira a couple of times. She was now crouched only a few metres away. Wamta looked up, a wide grin spreading across her face. She threw down her brush and rushed over to Saira.

"You came back!" Wamta said, extending her arms out for a hug. "You touched the notebook and, and…. just disappeared! I didn't think I'd ever see you again. Especially with your stone missing and all."

"I know, I know. I wasn't sure I'd be able to leave, or even to come back…You haven't found my stone yet, have you?" Saira asked.

Wamta shook her head. "Sorry Saira. I keep looking for it all the time, but we went so many places that day…"

Saira shrugged. "Maybe I don't even need it anymore? I mean, I got here without it, didn't I?"

"Yah, that's strange. Maybe you have some kind of magic power!" Wamta exclaimed, her brown eyes brightening.

"Haha! Yah, right! I wish," said Saira, turning towards the canoe. "What are you doing anyway?"

"This is part of our family crest," Wamta replied, grabbing Saira's hand and pulling her down closer. "Do you know what this is?" she asked playfully. She picked up her brush and dipped it back into the small pot of green paint.

Saira cocked her head to the side and walked around the front of the boat taking in all sides. "It actually kinda looks like a frog," she said pointing towards the webbed toes.

"You're right!" said Wamta, beaming with delight. "Those are the eyes — see how they're slanted up? And here, look, there are no eyebrows. That's the nose, and this here is the tongue," she said indicating the long, red section that dipped down towards the bottom of the canoe. "Frogs are spirit guides for canoes. Shaman, like the I'kinuxw, make their final journey to the spirit world in canoes. It's a very important symbol of passing from the earthly realm to the ocean realm. They can live on land or in the water."

"The frog is drinking from the sea?" asked Saira half-jokingly.

"Ha! Looks like that," replied Wamta. "But no, it's to show that the frog is giving knowledge and power to the water's world beings. The frog is very special for us. Highly respected. They are shaman helpers and can travel between the earth and spirit worlds."

"Wow. That's cool. And powerful," said Saira. "I'd like to be a frog."

"Cool?" said Wamta, giving Saira a strange look. "Yes, frogs *are* powerful. This canoe is dedicated to my brother. Remember, I told you his spirit animal is a frog. We can help keep his spirit alive by painting and carving his crest on sacred objects, like this canoe, and the totem pole up at the Big House entrance," she said, pointing up the hill. "They're also known to be great communicators and have amazing voices. They love to sing. My brother was exactly like that."

The more Saira learned, the more she was intrigued.

"This canoe is extra special, because it carries the soul of the cedar tree. Whatever people inside the boat feel, the canoe feels too!"

Saira reached her hand out to touch the boat. "Wait!" interrupted Wamta. "Don't touch it yet. It's not finished. The spirit has to rest until it's finished."

Saira whipped her hand back. "You know so much about your culture, Wamta. We're the same age and I know next to nothing about my own culture compared to you."

"It's only because we are losing so much of it… I'm trying to learn, and remember, as much as I can. I saw what the residential school did to my brother — he was forced to forget, or at least not practice any of it. That's motivated me to learn even more," explained Wamta.

Before Saira could respond, the voices from the boats started yelling. They were waving them over. "Wanna have some fun?" asked Wamta, her sparkle returning. "Looks like we're wanted in a canoe race!"

There were five canoes in the race. Each was painted with different animals representing different family crests. Saira and Wamta got in the same boat. It had two wolf-like serpent heads with curly horns and nostrils that splayed across each side of the bow. In the middle, the canoe's prow had a third face. It looked like a human with large, wide teeth and bulging eyes. Wamta explained this design was a two-headed snake that they called a sistiul or I-Hos and that it was a very powerful creature.

"It represents power and destruction. It protects the myth people," she said looking around. "We believe that bathing in the same waters give us a long and healthy life," she continued, passing Saira a cedar bark headband with large splaying feathers. Wamta then placed a hummingbird mask with a long, pointed nose on her own head.

This was the first time Saira had ever been in a canoe with so many people, let alone people dressed in colourful head dresses and animal masks. She reached into her pocket to take a photo, but felt only the medicine pouch and magic stone. *Nooo! I left the phone in Grandpapa's garden!*

"Are you OK?" asked Wamta seeing Saira's face.

"Oh, yah, no prob," answered Saira. She was kicking herself inside for forgetting her phone. How would she ever convince Nakawe that she time travelled again?

When the canoes got far enough from shore, they all swivelled their bows round and lined up. They were about to start the race. Saira was excited. She loved being on, or preferably *in* the water. Afterall, she was a Pisces, born on the 22nd of February. Her mom, who believed in astrology and the origins of the Zodiac, said that was why she loved the water so much.

Just then the paddling stopped. Everyone got very still. Then there was a burst of singing and clapping. "This is our Thunderbird Song. It's about brotherhood, sisterhood and family unity," Wamta explained.

From the shore, loud banging on drums started up and, before Saira knew it, they were in a canoe race. With every push of their paddles, the bow soared high up out of the water, then dove back down sending sprays of salt water over their faces. Saira felt a surge of adrenaline. She loved the exertion. She felt so free. In her mind, she started chanting, "heave, ho, heave, ho" though, in reality there was only the sound of the paddles cutting deep into the sea and propelling them forward. Wamta would occasionally glance back to exchange a quick smile from under her mask. Their team was battling with the eagle canoe for the lead.

"Let's get 'em!" Saira shouted up to Wamta. She was feeling giddy with competitiveness. But just as she went to sit back down, she slipped on the wooden floorboard and lost her balance. As she tried to steady herself with her paddle, she missed grabbing hold of the sideboards. She fell towards the boat's hull, knocked her forehead and sent her body hurling over the side plunging straight into the cold Pacific waters below.

All Saira remembered was a rush of frigid wetness ripple through her body and shoot deep into her lungs. There was the sound of panicked voices, the sight of colourful paddles splashing around underwater next to her and then nothing.

When Saira came around, she was swaying from side to side with the movement of the sea. All around she could see nothing but blurry hues of green and blue. Above her head, light streamed down bits of yellow and gold glimmers through the water. Her cedar bark headband and eagle feather gently slipped off and floated away. Saira reached out to grab it when she noticed her hand was actually a fin.

A giant frog swam by. "Don't worry about it," he said, turning his head towards Saira. "You'll get another one."

"Excuse me?" replied Saira. *How can I talk under water? And how is a frog even talking to me? He's not even moving his mouth!* "Another *what*?" she asked aloud.

"Another eagle feather, of course," replied the frog. His mouth remained motionless. He had stopped breast-stroking and was treading water with giant webbed feet. "Mother Eagle has been keeping her eye on you. I think you know that though, don't you?" he continued with a wink. "Anyway, you'll be meeting her – properly – very soon. It's a bit hectic in *Echuca* right now… She's currently resolving a dispute between a wolf and bear. But once that little mess is sorted, she'll be popping by your way."

"Huh? Mother Eagle? *Echuca*? What —? Where am I?" asked Saira, trying to rub her face with a slimy fin.

"Well, you're not exactly in the Gobi Desert," the frog replied. He was snorting with laughter through his flat nose. Little air bubbles spewed from his nostrils and floated upwards. "Welcome to the Coastal Salish sea! Call me Wakes. It means frog in Kwak'wala. I came down from Alert Bay."

Saira half expected him to extend his front legs to shake. "Gobi Desert? Wakes? Kwak'wala? Wait. Your name… it sounds… familiar," said Saira, furrowing her brows.

"You've obviously never been to Northern China or Southern Mongolia, then have you? That's the Gobi Desert," replied the frog, shaking his head in dismay. "And yes, Kwak'wala. It's the language of the Kwakwaka'wakw. You'll learn…As a *new* spirit animal you don't know as much about nature as we *veteran* spirit animals."

Saira just stared at Wakes dumbfounded. "Um...I'm Saira. How — how are you *speaking* without even moving your mouth?"

"Why would I move my mouth? Waste of energy, if you ask me," replied Wakes. His thick, red lips folded into a smile. "Spirit animals can speak with their minds.... Oh, you'll learn soon enough."

"OK... Do you live around—?" started Saira.

"Nope," Wakes interrupted. "Just a quick trip through. We, frogs, aren't exactly fans of salt water. Cinders our little feet to smithereens! Just passing through to give all you fish a message, while Mother Eagle is otherwise indisposed," he continued, flashing one of his four webbed fingers at Saira.

"All us *fish*?" Saira repeated.

"Yes. You — *salmon* — as well as the halibut, tuna and, of course, your close friends, the trout."

"O—K. So, what's the message, then?" Saira asked at last.

Wakes motioned above the water. "The message comes from the Great One. Up there. Mother Eagle sends a warning of secrets from the sky. Beware of the trickster raven. Protect your spirit family, dear one...Now, I must be off to tell the others."

Saira watched the glimmer of Wakes' green skin grown dim as he swam away. *Protect my spirit family? What is he talking about? Why am I a salmon? And what secrets does he mean?*

———◆———

"Saira? Hello? How are you feeling?"

Saira woke to see Wamta crouched overtop of her.

Saira coughed, then sputtered. As her pupils started to adjust, she could see the outline of a small crowd gathered round in a circle. A man with a long robe stood close by. It was yellow and white with a geometric grid-like pattern. His head was tilted back as he arched his torso to the sky. He was wearing an elaborate headdress adorned with feathers, skins, wood, quills, cedar bark and shells. There was a lone starfish hanging off to one side. Extending out from his face was a bird mask with a long beak and straggly bits of cedar bark that fell down around the mask. The man's eyes were closed, and he was chanting in a low monotone voice. In his right hand, was a pipe that he swayed from side to side like a music conductor. The long wool fringes from his robe moved rhythmically with his chant and smoke flowed out of the pipe, curling up into the air like a dancing snake. The scent of sacred herbs wafted through the air and filled Saira's nostrils.

"Where am I?" mumbled Saira. "Am I having another weird dream?" she continued in a daze.

"It's OK, Saira. You hit your head and fell over the boat. It was probably Iakim, the underwater monster. You're fine now."

"I-I-I was a fish," she continued. "I was underwater. A frog spoke to me. His name was Wakes, like your brother. He said something about family and secrets…"

Wamta passed Saira a small cup and propped her head up to drink. "Just rest and drink this. Breathe slowly…in…out…in… out…," she repeated resting the palm of her hand on Saira's forehead.

Saira took a small sip. The taste was bitter, but the warmth soothed her chest. She stretched down onto her back. High up in the sky she could see an eagle. It was circling round and round like a plane waiting to land. As she watched, she could see a small black dot fall from beneath the bird's wing. It weaved its way down through the sky, swaying from side to side before landing right next to Saira's face.

Wamta picked up the plume. It was taupe with dark flecks and an unusual speck of white at the very tip. "Lucky you!" she said. "Eagles are the Creator's most powerful birds. They symbolize good-luck and happiness. Make a wish, Saira. The feather will carry your prayer to the Creator."

Saira closed her eyes again and whispered to herself. *I wish my parents would stay together.* Then she opened them once more. "Wamta? Can I make two wishes?" she asked.

"I don't see why not," Wamta replied with a smile.

I wish Wamta would find her brother again, she said to herself before rolling onto her side and drifting back to sleep.

CHAPTER 13

It was the next day when Saira woke. She was inside the large plank house, where Wamta's family lived. A soft wooly blanket was wrapped around her and she could feel the warmth of the small, flickering fire nearby. Saira could see the silhouettes of Wamta and her mother huddled in a corner. They seemed to be weaving something. Her little sister was crawling around next to them.

"Good morning," said Wamta, looking over. "You slept a very long time. Your fall into the water gave you quite a scare, didn't it?"

"I guess so," said Saira. "It's so strange. I don't even know what happened!"

"Remember, things happen without explanation," said Wamta, her voice low. "Nature is more powerful than us."

"Kwa'tayu?" asked Wamta's mother, putting her hands to her eyebrow.

"No, abas, she should be OK," said Wamta to her mother. "She's worried about your cut."

"My cut? Why?" asked Saira, touching the tender bump over her left eyebrow.

"You'll be fine. Just keep the cold cloth on it for a bit. It'll keep the swelling down," reassured Wamta. "Here, this'll make you feel better. I made it for you last night." She passed a small circular object to Saira. "You were calling out in the night, something about your mom and dad. I think you were having a nightmare."

The ring was a couple inches wide. It was wrapped in black leather with a netting of fishing line woven through the middle. A single red bead was placed in the centre and dangling from the bottom was the small eagle feather that had fallen from the sky earlier.

Saira turned it over in her hands. "This is beautiful. What is it?"

"It's a Dream Catcher," explained Wamta, looking back up at her mom. "It's actually not from our culture. The Ojibwe make them, but I learned how to make it in school. I like the idea that it helps keep bad dreams away at night."

"I love it. Thank you," said Saira, giving it a squeeze before placing it into her pant pocket. She wanted to give Wamta something of her own, but what? She looked down at the colourful thread bracelet from Nakawe. She'd been wearing it for years now, but she knew Nakawe could make her another friendship bracelet. She carefully rolled it off her wrist. "Wamta," Saira said opening her hand. "I want you to have this. It's a friendship bracelet from Mexico. My best friend, Nakawe, made it for me. I know you two would get along, so I want you to have it."

Wamta let out a wide grin and quickly rolled the bracelet up around her own wrist. "Thank you, Saira," she said rolling the threads between her fingers. "Red is my favourite colour. Friends forever, then."

———— • ————

For breakfast, Wamta showed Saira how to make fry bread. They mixed together flour, baking powder, salt, and water in a large wooden bowl. Then, they pounded the dough into a big ball before tearing off bits to make smaller balls that they stretched and rolled out flat. Then they filled a pan with lard and placed it over the fire. The oil crackled and popped as it began frying up the bread. By the time it was ready, Saira was famished. It smelled so good. They dipped the fry bread in some leftover eulachon oil from Wakes' celebration of life ceremony.

Between mouthfuls of bread, Wamta invited Saira to her Talking Circle later that day. "You can meet other people from my tribe. Auntie Evelyn is one of the elders who is running it today," she explained, wiping crumbs of fry bread from her lips. "Do you know what a Talking Circle is?"

Saira shook her head and smiled. "Wamta, I think by now you must realize I know pretty much zilch about your culture."

"Zilch?" asked Wamta.

"Sorry, I mean 'nothing'… I keep forgetting we actually live in completely different times and we use some totally different words," Saira continued with a giggle.

"Ha ha, true!" said Wamta. "It's OK, I don't expect you to know about my culture. We're the ones who are *supposed* to be learning about your culture, I guess," Wamta continued turning away. "Talking Circles are not really from our Coast Salish or Kwakwaka'wakw cultures. It's from another Indigenous group, but we use it here because we've found it helpful. It's a group of young people, just like us, that meet once a month. It's organized by a couple of the elders. They're the circle keepers."

"OK…" said Saira a bit uncertainly.

"We sit in a circle and each takes turn holding the Talking Stick. It goes around counterclockwise, like the moon around the earth. Then whoever holds the stick gets to speak."

Saira nodded. It was sounding interesting.

"It's nice to sit this way, because then you can see everyone in front of you. And you're supposed to listen. You can't interrupt until it's your turn to hold the Talking Stick," Wamta added.

"Sounds easy enough. And what do you talk about?" asked Saira.

"It's usually something personal, but you can talk about anything really…or nothing too, if that's what you prefer. You just say 'pass' and we move on to the next person."

"You're sure it's OK if I join?" continued Saira. "I mean, what if they find out I'm not from here? They won't know that I come from the future, but you know... I think they'll see that I'm... well, I'm different."

"Don't worry about that. Anyone can join. Really. It's supposed to be a safe place. Every person is equal and every person belongs. The only important thing to remember is that what's said during the circle *stays* in the circle," said Wamta, as the two girls finished their last bites of breakfast.

The Talking Circle took place in a different plank house. When Wamta and Saira walked in, there were already some half a dozen other kids waiting. There was no reason Saira would be considered an outsider. Every colour of hair, eye and skin tone was there, though Saira was the only one barefoot. She had been wearing her flip flops, because she didn't have any other shoes other than the Converse she'd left at the potlatch, but Wamta told her to leave them at her house. "Those are definitely not of our times," she said.

"Gilakas'la, Wamta," greeted an elderly woman when the two girls entered. She took Wamta's hand in both her hands. She had a wide, toothy smile that stretched and sparkled across her entire face. She stood about five feet tall.

"Gilakas'la, Auntie," responded Wamta with a slight bow of her head. "This is my friend Saira. She's from out of town. Would it be OK if she joined us today?"

"It is our pleasure," said Auntie Evelyn looking to Saira. "Please, you are welcome into our Circle. Did Wamta explain how it works?"

"Yes," said Saira. "And Gilakas'la. I'm really happy to be here."

Another elder, this one a man, called everyone to come together. He was holding a metre-long cedar staff in the air. It was fully carved and painted in red, green, white and black. It reminded Saira of a mini totem pole. The only design on the staff that Saira recognized was an eagle. It stood at the very top, its wings spread out wide.

The kids gathered round, including Wamta and Saira, and they all sat cross-legged on the dirt floor. The two elders stood at opposite ends of the Circle.

"We have a new friend with us today," announced the man looking over at Saira. "Gilakas'la, Saira."

Saira smiled, though she could feel her face turning crimson as everyone turned to look at her.

"Gilakas'la," she said looking down.

The man passed the stick over to Auntie Evelyn. "Today we'd like to center our Circle discussion on the topic of youth," she said, looking each person carefully in the eye. "You are our future," she continued, pointing the stick. "You are our greatest resource and we cherish you all. We'd like to hear about what being a young Indigenous person today, in 1941, means to you. We have some Kwakwaka'wakw, Coast Salish and Nuu-chah-nulth here, but we are all one. Remember there is no right or wrong. There's only your thoughts, what you feel and how you choose to share them, *if* you choose to share today."

Auntie paused for a few moments. She looked around the Circle again studying each face. Saira felt calm, though she couldn't shake the feeling that someone was watching her from behind. She tried to turn her head round, but all she saw was the quick flutter of a bird's wing.

"Would anyone like to start?" asked Auntie Evelyn.

Wamta raised her hand. "I will." Auntie passed the staff to Wamta. She took it with both hands and cleared her throat. "As you all know, we had my brother's celebration of life ceremony recently. He's gone to another world," she began. Saira could tell she was choosing her words. "And now — now that he has gone, I am the next child in line for my family. My abad always told me that education offers opportunity, but I always believed this education was about my people and culture. But now I've been told that I have to go to Port Alberni, like my brother did, to go to the residential school."

There was a long pause. Everyone was looking down. Saira could see the bottom part of her friend's chin trembling, and both of her hands, clutched around the staff, were starting to shake. She reached over and placed her hand on her friend's knee.

"I — I'm not looking forward to it. At all. Maybe I should be grateful for getting an education? But from the stories I've heard, I'm scared. I don't want to go. We are not allowed to be who we are. I am feeling very alone and…and… I'm not even gone yet." Wamta put the Talking Stick down and covered her face with the cup of her hands. The sound of her tears was muffled, and her back was quivering.

Auntie Evelyn came over and picked up the Stick. She wrapped her arms around Wamta. "Thank you for sharing. We are feeling your pain alongside you. We all know someone who has gone away to these schools. It is very sad. All we can do is promise to do our best to ensure you keep your Indigenous identity and culture alive whenever you come home to visit."

The Circle rested in silence for a minute, then Auntie gave a smile of encouragement to Saira and extended the cedar staff. The bruise on Saira's eyebrow started to throb as she reached out to take the Stick. And as soon as her fingertips touched the wood, she felt what had now become a familiar sensation. Her body began to tingle. Her fingers grew numb, her heart began to race and pressure started mounting in her head. Her eyes grew painfully heavy and her entire world went from blotchy white to completely black.

CHAPTER 14

When Saira finally opened her eyes, she was lying in a heap of soil in her Grandpapa's garden, exactly where she'd been after touching the spindle whorl. Her phone laid covered in dirt nearby. In the past world she'd been away for a couple days, but in the present world Grandpapa was still not home. His car wasn't even in the driveway.

Oh no! I took their Talking Stick, Saira thought looking down at the wooden staff still clutched in her hands. *Wamta is definitely not going to be happy about this.*

In her pocket, Saira felt Wamta's dreamcatcher. This comforted her. But she knew she had to get upstairs, and fast, before anyone saw her. She quickly filled the hole where she'd found the spindle whorl then made a dash for the house gripping the wooden staff like a relay baton. Once in her room, she slammed the door and plopped herself down on the carpet. Her heart was pounding. She pulled out her phone: *Nak, I did it again! But NOT with the totem pole. Talk??*

Nakawe immediately called her on video chat. "What do you mean, chica? Geez, what did you do to your eyebrow?" she cried, pointing at Saira's image on her phone.

"I almost forgot," said Saira touching the cut above her eye. "I fell off a boat. I was in a canoe race."

"In a *what?*" cried Nakawe. "Where? Are you telling me you went into the past world again? What happened to the totem pole? How'd you get —?"

"Woah, woah. Wait. Slow down! I have so much to tell you." Saira recounted what happened since they'd last messaged. Her head was swirling with all the events and emotions. There was so much to fill her in on, starting with the missing totem pole, watching Tooan and Satsam dig around in the garden, then traveling back in time with the spindle whorl. She told Nakawe about the canoe race, meeting Wakes, the talking frog, and the old man with the eagle feather. She finally finished by explaining the Talking Circle and touching the wooden staff that sent her hurling back into the present world. "I almost forgot. I got this," she explained pulling out the dreamcatcher. "It's to help with these strange dreams I've been having."

"Cool!" replied Nakawe, pulling the phone closer to her face.

"And Nak, I gave Wamta the friendship bracelet from you. It was a present — kinda from us both," she explained. "I hope you don't mind?"

"Course not. It's getting to see the world… And time travelling now too, ha ha! I'll make you another one, don't worry," said Nakawe, before pausing. "But I'm still confused. How did you time travel without the totem pole?" Nakawe had a puzzled, serious look on her face. Saira had seen that look before. She was deep in thought. Finally, she asked Saira to send her a photo of all the clues she brought back from the past world. "There must be something in those objects that we are missing," Nakawe said biting her lip.

Just before bed, Saira pulled out the three past world objects. There was the wooden bowl, the leather notebook and, now, the Talking Stick. She examined each one carefully, then lined them up on the bedspread to take some photos for Nakawe: *Here u go! This is what I took from past world. Talk 2morrow*

———◆———

Saira didn't hear Grandpapa come home that evening. Even though her mind was racing, she had no problem falling to sleep within seconds of her head hitting the pillow. At around midnight, she woke with a start to a rattling sound at the window.

Edging out of her bed, Saira inched forward and pulled back the curtain. The window was partially open. A warm August breeze brushed in, tickling her face. But she still couldn't see anything. She pushed the window open a tiny bit more and peered out over the sill. Two small, yellow circles emerged from the darkness and a curved beak knocked up against the pane.

"Aaaahh!" Saira cried, leaping back.

"Hmmbbbaaa," the bird started in a slow, dignified tone. It sounded like she was tuning her voice, but there was no movement from her beak. "Don't be scared. I'm Mother Eagle," she continued, her beak held high.

She seemed to have a slight accent, but Saira couldn't tell where it was from. Her voice was calm and reassuring. Like Wakes, her voice seemed to emanate from her entire body.

"Hmmbbbaaa. We nearly met after your spill in the water the other day. It was me who sent you the small feather," she continued, indicating towards the dreamcatcher by her bed. The bird hopped a bit further through the window so that one wing was drooping casually over the ledge. She scoured Saira's room, as if scouting for someone else.

"Did — did I hit my head again?" asked Saira, feeling for the bruise on her eyebrow. It was starting to sting like a cut.

"I believe you have been expecting me," said Mother Eagle, one eyelid slightly arched. "Wakes should have told you." Saira still looked stunned. "You met Wakes in Echuca recently, hmmbbbaaa?" Mother Eagle continued. Her voice was matter-of-fact as she waved her left wing around.

"Wakes?" Saira asked perplexed. "Echuca?"

"Yes. Wakes. Don't tell me you forgot about him? Oh, that poor old frog. I certainly won't tell him that. You met him when you fell underwater. Remember your canoe race with Wamta? That's when we transported you into Echuca."

She couldn't believe she were having a conversation with an eagle, let alone one that knew about her time travels and Wamta.

Mother Eagle could see that she was taken aback. "Hmmbbbaaa, Echuca means the meeting of the waters," Mother Eagle emitted, ruffling her feathers with vague annoyance. "I thought Wakes would have told you when you were underwater with him…. It's where you've been travelling in your dreams. Except these are not *actually* dreams. You were born with this ability and now you have been officially marked," she continued pointing towards Saira's eyebrow. "Don't be alarmed. I can see you are slowly piecing together parts of the puzzle."

"The puzzle?" asked Saira.

"The disappearance of Wakes' human form from the past," explained Mother Eagle. "We all have our animal spirits, but very few are in touch with both their human and animal sides… But you —*you* are." Her stare was so intense it was making Saira uncomfortable.

"I — I am?"

"Of course, hmmbbbaaa. Look closely at the objects that hold the animal spirits captive. Look closely at your visions in Echuca."

"What animal spirits? What visions?" asked Saira, rubbing at her eyelids.

And just like that, Mother Eagle flung her head back round towards the sky and pushed herself off the sill with her talons. Saira was left standing alone under the midnight moon, her mouth agape.

The next morning Saira was sure she'd dreamed the entire episode with Mother Eagle. *It couldn't possibly have been real… could it?*

She checked her phone. Nakawe had left a message on WhatsApp voice: "Hola chica, I hope you don't mind but I showed my aya your picture. I just told her it was for a summer school project. She asked about the material and design. It's all wood, right? Do you know what kind? And can you send some close-ups? We need to see the crests on each object. How's your cut? It looked totally messed up last night. Gotta run. Hasta luega, chica! Besos!"

Saira felt her eyebrow. It was pulsating. She looked in the wardrobe mirror. Sure enough, the cut looked worse. "Is it growing?" she whispered looking back at her reflection. She wished she had some skin foundation like her mother used on special occasions. This was going to be hard to explain...

The scent of fried eggs and bacon wafting up through the floor vent interrupted her thoughts.

———————•———————

Saira was nervous to see Grandpapa. Living between the past and present was starting to confuse her, but she didn't want to let on what was happening. She quickly threw on her t-shirt and jeans and hid her dreamcatcher in her bedside table drawer. She also stored the notebook, bowl and Talking Stick back in the pillow case and pushed it to the very back of the closet.

When Saira got downstairs, she was surprised to see Tooan and Satsam at the table. Tooan was flipping through some papers. Satsam was picking at a hangnail.

"Hi," she said, meekly stepping into the kitchen. She still felt guilty about begin caught trying on the mask the other day.

"Hi Sai—," said Tooan, stopping when he saw her eyebrow.

"What the heck happened to your bruise?" asked Satsam, his face a mixture of amusement and horror.

Grandpapa turned his head away from the frying pan and looked equally shocked. "Saira! What happened?" he cried, throwing down the flipper. His look made Saira think her cut actually looked far worse in the kitchen light.

"Oh, this?" Saira answered casually, placing a finger ever so gently over the cut. "It's nothing. Really. Just a small cut from a…a tree branch that I walked into yesterday."

"A tree branch did that?" repeated Grandpapa, before shooting Tooan a worried look. "You have to be careful, Saira. It might be infected there. Satsam, please show her where the band aids are in the bathroom. I need to finish up with breakfast here."

"Yah, sure," mumbled Satsam, in no rush to push himself up from the table. "Follow me, Saira."

The two headed towards the bathroom at the end of the hall. As they walked past the room opposite Grandpapa's office, Saira noticed a red box on the floor. She hadn't seen this box before, and it was wide open. She peered down just long enough to catch sight of a loose photo sticking up from the pile. It was slightly yellowed and starting to curl up at the corners. There were three people in the picture, but there was something very strange about this photo. Saira reached down to grab it. She could make out a younger, much skinnier version of Grandpapa. He was wearing his standard outfit — Carhartt utility pants and his black bucket hat. He was standing next to a beautifully carved totem pole with two young kids on either side – a boy and a girl, maybe around Saira's age. Her gaze moved to the image of the girl. She heart stopped.

CHAPTER 15

It was uncanny. The girl in the photograph, it was definitely Wamta. The same almond shaped eyes, high cheekbones and jet-black hair pulled back in a ponytail. But why was she standing with Grandpapa? And a younger version, at that? And who was this young boy with them? Was it Wamta's missing brother? When was this photograph taken? How do they know each other?

All these questions swirled around in Saira's head like a typhoon. She was sitting on the floor in her bedroom. Her face was deeply flush and her cut had gone from stinging to tingly and numb. She'd told Satsam that she felt tired and was going to nap. She pulled the photograph out again. There was no doubt, it was Grandpapa, several decades ago. He was wearing the very same black bucket hat. It was a lot newer back then. She pulled the wooden bowl, leather notebook and Talking Stick out again from the back of the closet and propped them up on her mattress. She picked up the bowl, twisting and turning it round in her hand. She leaned the bowl on its side to closely examine the design. It was a creature of some sort, but what? It had a flat nose, slanted eyes, no eyebrows and big wide lips with a squiggly tongue curling down into another creature that looked like a fish.

This must be a frog, Saira thought, tracing her fingertips over the face. *It's just like the design on the canoe stern, which was Wamta's brother's spirit animal.*

Next, Saira picked up the small, brown, leather notebook and carefully ran her fingers across the embossed crest on the front. It was still very much intact, and she could clearly see that it, too, had the very same design on the front— a frog with what looked to be a fish extending down from its tongue. She reached for the Talking Stick. Again, there it was — the same two creatures carved into the bottom of the staff. All three objects had the same animal symbols. But what did this mean?

How does it all fit together? Saira wondered. *Wamta said something about frogs being shaman helpers and their tongues sharing knowledge with other creatures…*

Saira stood up and went to the window. She looked out over the backyard as she began tapping her bottom lip. *I wonder if the totem pole and spindle whorl have the same design? I need to go back and see Wamta. I need to find another object with a similar design. But where in the world will I find that?*

⸻ ◆ ⸻

Eventually Saira went back downstairs — her stomach was going to eat itself from the inside if she didn't. By that time, Tooan and Satsam had already left and Grandpapa was working in his office. She could hear him coughing. He was sounding worse every day.

With her phone, Saira took a picture of the photograph she'd found in the red box, then tucked it away in the drawer of her bedside table next to her dreamcatcher. She sent the image to Nakawe and tried calling, but there was no answer. She was eager to tell her about meeting Mother Eagle, the latest discovery with the photograph and her suspicions about the carved designs.

Nakawe didn't respond until the late afternoon. She was back from a hike in the mountains and wanted to video chat. "My god, chica! What is happening with your cut?" Nakawe shouted, pointing to Saira's face.

"With everything going on, I almost forgot to tell you," said Saira. "That bruise I got — you know when I fell in the water — well, it has somehow become a cut. It's so weird. That's not even the important thing. So much has happened since yesterday."

Saira filled Nakawe in on meeting with Mother Eagle and Echuca. "Did you see the photograph I sent you?" asked Saira, her eyebrows raised.

"Yah, I did. It's hard to really see. I don't know. Not sure what's so important about this," said Nakawe. "I mean, it's your Grandpapa with a couple kids, right?"

"Yes. It is my Grandpapa. And I don't know who the boy is. But the girl, Nak, the *girl* — that is my friend Wamta! You know, the one from the past?"

"Huh? What? Just sec," answered Nakawe, moving the phone up closer to her face. "O-o-o-ok," she said under her breath. "Are you sure? I mean, it could just be someone who looks similar... Like, how can this even be possible?"

"No idea. I mean, I guess you could be right... Maybe it *is* a mistake," Saira said finally. "I mean, if my Grandpapa is with Wamta then does that mean that *he* also time travelled? Or was it *Wamta* that time travelled? And who is *this boy*? Her brother? I am totally confused." She paused. "I also noticed that the three objects I took back from the past, they all have the same design. It's like a family crest or something."

Nakawe tilted her head.

"And I think...I *think* both the totem pole and spindle whorl have the same crests too. I'm not totally positive, Nak, but I do have to find another object with the same design to see... because *if* it lets me travel back again then I know for sure. I know that there is something magical about this crest. And then — *then* I can ask Wamta about this photo," explained Saira. She was starting to pace the room like a caged lion.

"I have an idea, chica," said Nakawe. "You said you travelled back with a spindle whorl last time, right? The one you found buried in the garden? Well, if *that* was buried there, maybe it's because whoever buried it there *knows* it has powers?

"Hmmmm, or maybe it's me that has powers!" said Saira half-jokingly, as she looked out the window at the garden. "That's it, Nak! I have to go back. I do! I'm going back tonight."

— • —

Saira waited until several hours after dinner, when she knew Grandpapa would be back in his office for the evening, or maybe even have fallen asleep. Saira could often hear him snoring through the floorboards below.

All day Saira had the jitters. She was anxious to go back to the garden. She'd exchanged with Nakawe again on her plan. She'd already snuck a hand shovel from the shed into her room. She would try to find another buried wooden object in the garden – one with the same frog and salmon crest. She needed to see Wamta again and find out if this really was her in the photograph. And if it *was*, then how did she know Grandpapa? And *who* was this young boy with them?

At around midnight, Saira made sure her phone was safely stored in the pocket of her cargo pants, along with the photograph in her zip pocket. She grabbed her flashlight from her backpack and, as she was riffling through to get it, noticed the red envelope from her mother. She had forgotten all about it. She placed it by her pillow so she could read it later. There was too much on her mind right now.

Outside, the moon was full and bright. It was like a disco ball radiating across the trees and grass. She tiptoed towards the garden, turning on the flashlight only once she reached the plots. She couldn't shake the feeling that she was being watched. At one point she looked up and swore she saw large, round eyes and the outline of a short, hooked beak in the cedar tree above her. It was probably an owl, but it flew away too quickly, making little more than a couple fluttering sounds in the trees.

Saira wasn't exactly sure where to start digging, so she just pointed her shovel down and began. *If other objects, like the spindle whorl, are buried here, then it shouldn't take too long to find them,* she thought as she continued lifting out small mounds of soil.

Sure enough, after a few minutes she felt the clunk of her shovel against a hard object. *Yes, I hit something!* She crouched down to the soil and propped the flashlight between her knees. Brushing away the dirt, she could see a small, wooden hand rattle. As she pulled it out, she braced herself for the tingly sensation and blackout she'd now grown accustomed to. But there was nothing. She opened her eyes again and looked around. Her heart sank.

She let out a deep sigh, then looked down to better examine the rattle in her hands. The carving looked similar, but there was one difference. There didn't seem to be any kind of fish coming off the end of the frog's tongue. *Ok, so this one doesn't work,* she thought grabbing her shovel and moving on to the next pile of dirt.

Another few minutes passed. Saira worked quickly, flinging up soil high into the air. Suddenly the back-porch light flicked on and Grandpapa's profile appeared on the patio. Saira panicked. She pushed the flashlight down into the dirt to block the light just as her shovel clunked against another hard object.

"Saira? Saira, is that you?"

She could hear her Grandpapa's raspy voice as she reached down to touch the unknown surface. Then, as her fingers wrapped around the hard, cold material, she felt the familiar prickly feeling creep up into her fingers, hands, arms and then flood through her entire body. Then everything, as expected, turned to black.

CHAPTER 16

The familiar smell of smudge, cedar and salt water filled Saira's nostrils. She got up and wiped her face with the back of her hand. She was still holding the carved, wooden rattle in her hands. The very same frog and fish crest was etched onto this object too. *Yep, there is definitely something about this design,* she thought.

Looking around, she could see she was back inside the Big House, exactly where she'd arrived when she first time-travelled into the potlatch. But this time, there was no one else around, just the quiet sounds of rain tickling the ground outside. *I need to find Wamta right away,* Saira thought heaving through the front doors.

Once outside, she could see people down by the water. Most seemed to be heading back to their homes, as the rain was starting to come down hard. Saira set off for Wamta's family house.

When she walked in, she headed straight to Wamta's mom who was sitting in her usual spot, on a cedar bark mat by the fire, with her baby.

"Gilakas'la," she said, turning around, her face brightening.

"Gilakas'la," echoed Saira.

"Kwaga'lił," said Wamta's mom, gesturing for her to sit down.

Saira then realized talking with her would be next to impossible. She smiled and took a seat anyway. Wamta's baby sister looked up from breastfeeding and waved her tiny hand towards Saira's face. Saira leaned in, letting the baby tap on her nose. She giggled. Wamta's mom smiled as her baby cooed.

"Petah," said Wamta's mother, nodding and pointing to her little girl.

"Is that her name? She must be over ten months then now?" Saira said before pausing. "Hey. That's funny...That was my grandmother's name too. Maybe it's a common name?"

Wamta's mom looked blankly at Saira, then offered another smile. Clearly, she had no idea what she was saying.

"Wamta?" Saira asked, shrugging her shoulders as she looked around the room.

"Atłi," responded Wamta's mom.

Saira scratched her head. "Cooking?" she asked, gesturing the stirring of a pot.

Wamta's mom shook her head. "Atłi," she repeated a bit louder, as if saying it more loudly would help her understand.

"Outside?" Saira asked, pointing towards the door.

"Am," nodded Wamta's mom stretching her arms up into a V-shape.

"Forest?"

Wamta's mom looked confused. She continued to point outside and repeated, "Am".

"OK, thanks. I'm going to look for her," said Saira, before giving Petah a quick tickle on her cheek then heading for the door. "Gilakas'la, again."

When Saira stepped outside she had no idea where to start venturing, but she had to start fast. The rain was falling in buckets. She double-checked her pockets to make sure both her phone and the photograph were still there. Then she set off in the direction of the forest, along the same path they'd been to pick berries before.

Entering into the woods, she had that uneasy feeling again. It was like she was being followed, but when she looked up all she could see were branches swaying in the wind.

Saira picked up her pace. "Wamta?" she cried out. The only response was a small hummingbird fluttering next to her head. "You are beautiful, aren't you?" whispered Saira, as she watched the little bird buzz in place. She extended her hand, inviting it to land. She'd seen so few since arriving at Grandpapa's. After a few seconds of flitting around her fingertips, the hummingbird finally landed on the very tip of her index finger. Saira let out a very slow breath, then leaned in. It was so delicate and graceful.

Suddenly a loud rattle, followed by a high-pitched caw shot down from above. The hummingbird scurried off. "Urgh!" said Saira looking up to the treetops. She could see a raven peering down. Then she heard some voices. It was hard to tell where they were coming from exactly. The sound of the rain hitting the tree branches was making it hard to hear. Saira could barely make out the words: "…come…safe…together…"

Straining to hear, she crept forward along the trail. Though the words were muffled, one of the tones sounded strangely familiar. It wasn't Wamta. It was a male voice. She continued creeping forward and tucked down behind a large cedar tree. Peering around the trunk she could see the outlines of two people standing just a few metres away. One was very tall, dressed in dark clothing. She couldn't see the other person. *Oh my god, maybe it really is the Wild Woman of the Woods*, thought Saira. The skin on her arms was starting to prickle.

Another voice started up. "Where have you…? Who is …?"

Saira crept closer, crouching low to the ground. A small frog startled her as it jumped across her face, but she remained focused. She held her breath, but her heart was going wild. Now one of the other voices did sound like Wamta. She sounded excited and scared at the same time. Then came an older man's voice. It was coming from a bit further away. His tone was dry, stern even. Again, he too sounded distinctly familiar. Saira squinted hard as she pushed away a few branches from view. She could only see the bottom pant legs of the taller person and Wamta's leather moccasins. She knew there was a third person standing a few metres away, but she couldn't see

121

them. He or she seemed to be behind a giant cedar tree. Saira wasn't even sure Wamta could see who it was.

She strained to get closer, but the underbrush blocking her way was just too thick. As she took a small step forward, something slid up her leg. A small, white snake was winding its way up her calf, his tongue slithering in and out. She let out an enormous yelp. "Uuuuuuggghhh!" she screamed, running out of the shrubs her arms flailing.

The voices suddenly stopped.

"Saira!" cried Wamta running towards her friend. "What are you —?"

Saira halted and looked up. She blinked hard. Whoever the other two people were, they were wearing large, wooden face masks. One was wearing a massive bird mask with wings outstretched horizontally, nearly a metre on each side. Saira couldn't make out the second one, but she did see a flash of green and big bulging eyes. When they heard Saira's cry, both masks snapped shut. Then, just as suddenly, they vanished into two huge swirls of smoke that wound their way up through the trees, disappearing into the evening sky.

———— ·◆· ————

When Saira finally recovered from her shock, she knelt down next to Wamta who was on her knees. "I—I don't understand," she said between whimpers. "I'm sure that was my brother. But I don't know who he was *with* — it wasn't Tal, I know that much, but I don't know who it was. They were both wearing transformation masks and I think...I think they were trying to *take me away*. But I don't know why... and I don't know where."

Saira put her arm around Wamta. She was trembling. "You're OK. You're safe now." The truth was, Saira was also scared and confused. Out of the corner of her eye, she could see a huge set of footprints in the mud right under the cedar tree. "I think we should go back to your house. It's probably not a good idea to stay here in the woods… you know, in case they come back. I also want to talk to you about something… well, to show you something really," she continued, feeling for the photograph in her pant pocket.

Wamta looked up at her friend, her face still pale with fright. "Ok, let's go. But please, don't mention this to anyone. I don't want my ada to get more worried then she already is."

When the girls got back to the plank house, as much as Wamta tried to put on a brave face her mom could see that she was upset. She brought a Chilkat blanket over and wrapped it around her shoulders. Wamta didn't say anything. She just spoke some words Saira didn't understand. Her mom then went back to the fire where she was frying some dough.

"Wamta, I'd like to show you something, if now's OK?" said Saira, her tone soft. "I found this photograph at my Grandpapa's — in the future — well, my present, but you know what I mean."

"Sure, OK. What is it?" answered Wamta.

Saira pulled out the old photograph from her pant pocket and leaned in. Both girls stared at the image. But there were now only two people in the photograph: Grandpapa and the young boy. "Oh my god," said Saira. "This can't be!"

"Hey, where did you get this?" said Wamta, simultaneously pulling the photograph from Saira's hands.

"This is crazy!" continued Saira.

"This is my brother! But who is this man?" she asked, pointing to Grandpapa.

Both girls looked at each other wide eyed and confused.

"You — you will never believe this, but there was actually a third person in this photo. That person was you," said Saira.

"Wha—?" Wamta was about to respond when her mom interrupted to give them a couple pieces of fresh fry bread. She extended the wooden plate to Saira. Just as she wrapped her fingers around the wood, her fingertips went numb and she felt the tingled in her arms. Then her world went black.

CHAPTER 17

Saira woke with dirt in her mouth. "Ugh!" she spat, then wiped her lips. She was back at Grandpapa's, in his garden. Gripped around her fingers was the wooden plate from Wamta's mother. Before she could take a closer look, a dry, gruff voice called from behind her.

"Who's there? Come out! I know you're there!" She looked up to see Grandpapa a couple of feet away. He was holding a flashlight and trampling through his garden wearing big, clunky work boots and his bucket hat, even though it was nighttime.

Why is he ignoring me? wondered Saira.

Grandpapa was now standing directly over-top of her. She was squatting on the soil, too scared to look up or even to breathe. Her stomach fizzed and clenched. She started counting silently in her head. The seconds felt like hours, but finally Grandpapa took another step, away from Saira. He was headed back towards the garden shed. *What is he doing? It's like...like he can't see me. Or... or...it's like I'm not even here.*

She bit her bottom lip hard. As soon as Grandpapa turned his head, Saira took a deep breath then sprinted for the house, clutching the wooden plate close to her hip. When she got inside her room, she flicked on the light and looked down at the wooden plate in her hands. It was exactly the same frog and fish as all the other objects that allowed her to time travel. *Amazing,* thought Saira. *So, it is the design! This crest really is magic!*

When her breathing returned to normal, she looked up. But it wasn't her room. There were bookshelves on all sides piled high to the ceiling. A beige chaise lounge was positioned in the corner with a foot stool and antique floor lamp. A large, glass coffee table was next to the chaise lounge, as was a rocking chair and magazine rack. The walls were covered with a series of framed photos and pastel watercolour paintings. There was no bed and no bedside table. Saira was paralyzed. For a second, she thought she must be in the wrong house. But there was the same closet. She opened it to see if her stuff was still in there. Nothing. No backpack. No letter from her mom. And most certainly no wooden bowl, leather notebook or Talking Stick. It was as if nothing from her present existed as she remembered. It was as if Saira's life didn't actually exist at all.

"What is going on?" she whispered under her breath. Her heart was racing.

As she closed the closet door she was again startled by a light rapping at the windowsill. She got to her knees, scared of what it might be. When she turned her head, she saw the familiar outline of a curved beak poised up against the pane. "Mother Eagle?" squeaked Saira. "Is that you?"

"Hmmbbbaaa. A fine mess you've made, Saira," said Mother Eagle, her tone accusatory.

"Excuse me?" whispered Saira. "What — what do you mean?"

"You have to be careful. Interfering with the past world affects the future. And affecting the future means affecting you," she said pointing her long, speckled wing at Saira.

Saira was still confused. Mother Eagle seemed to be almost rolling her eyes with annoyance. "I'm not used to spelling these things out, but looks like you need the help. You're new and all," she said frankly. She looked at the wooden plate, now laying on the carpet by the door. "Look, you've surely understood your powers by now. You must also realize that you've done something quite… well, quite *stupid*, to be honest. You need to be careful when you time travel." Mother Eagle paused for a moment letting her words sink in. "Hmmbbbaaa. You kept Wamta from travelling into the present, which means, that you — Saira Amara Lapierre — you no longer exist in this earthly realm."

Saira's jaw dropped. "What?" The wooden plate slipped from her hands, falling onto the hardwood floor. "What does this mean? You mean… I'm — I'm dead?"

———— ◆ ————

"Don't panic. You're hardly dead," explained Mother Eagle, starting to pluck tiny bits of lint from her feathers. "But you are not alive in the human form."

Saira was dumbfounded. "Not — not in a *human* form? What does this even mean?" she asked, standing up to see her reflection in the night window. Staring back at her were two big eyes, a hooked mouth and red and white scaly skin. "What *is* this?" she cried, putting her hand up to the reflection in the windowpane. "Oh my god! Am I a…*a salmon?*"

Mother Eagle let out a heavy sigh. "My goodness, dear! We've been telling you that for days now. Your dreams… remember? Don't worry, no one else sees you as a salmon. We need to fix this situation — that is *if* you want to be alive in the earthly realm too?"

Saira's head bobbed up and down.

"Ok, so it's really quite straightforward. Where is the purple vile I gave you?"

Saira gave another confused look. "You mean, that was *you*. You – *you* are I'kinuxw?"

Mother Eagle let out a slight smile. "Hmmbbbaaa, Saira, now you're getting it. So…do you have it?"

"Well, I did," started Saira, clearing her throat. She suddenly forgot entirely where she put the vile. "I mean, I stored my things at the back of the closet here," she said pointing to where the bedroom closet used to be. "But it looks like that's gone now."

Mother Eagle cocked her head and pursed her beak. "There's only one thing we can do, then."

"What's that?"

"You'll need to come with me to Echuca straight away so we can get you some more. But before we go through with that journey, I need to be sure you're ready for what this means?"

Saira hesitated. "Ok…What does this mean?"

"When you drink the purple liquid, you drink your destiny. You accept the gift that has been passed down to you from your uncle."

Saira's throat felt dry and itchy. "But — I don't have an uncle," she started. "Both my parents are only children."

Mother Eagle smiled. "Hmmbbbaaa, my dear, you are about learn a whole lot more about your family," she said. "But first, let me ask you once more. Are you ready to accept your powers and all that comes with it?"

Saira paused and looked down. "I —I guess so… I mean, what choice do I have, really?"

"Then hold on! We're going on a little trip."

And with that Saira took hold of Mother Eagle's wing and the two of them fled up into the night sky.

When they arrived, Saira initially thought they were back in the forest near Grandpapa's. But the light was not the same. It was extraordinarily bright, almost painfully so. And it was multi-coloured; rays of blue, red, green, yellow, orange and purple splayed off in all directions like refractive crystal. She looked up and saw towering cedar and Sitka spruce swaying in the wind. But there was something curious about these trees. They weren't just towering. They were very, very high. So high she couldn't even see the tops. They were like natural skyscrapers, each ledge of branches serving as another floor that ascended into the clouds. She rolled over and realized she was laying on a massive moss duvet. It was so spongy and soft, like millions and millions of goose feathers padded beneath her. An enormous ant scurried past her nose. She gasped, then swallowed. The humid air left a pungent taste of salt water at the back of her throat. She exhaled then took another deep breath in. Her nostrils filled with an overwhelming earthly scent of soil, salt and cedar. All around, she could hear the wind rustling through the trees. Combined with the powerful caws of far off ravens, the chirping of crickets and a loud single soft-pitched note of an eagle overhead, it was like a symphony of nature.

"Hmmbbbaaa. You feeling OK?" said a familiar voice.

Saira looked up to see Mother Eagle peering down from atop an enormous tree stump. "Guess so," replied Saira. "Did we make it? Are we — are we in Echuca?"

"Welcome!" said Mother Eagle, hopping closer to Saira's face. "I don't imagine you'll feel too out of sorts here. It's pretty much like the earthly world, though you won't find any human forms here. Just lush flora and fauna. There's nothing to kill us off. Though there are actually some forms, like you, living here. Forms that can live across both worlds," she continued, waving her wing around as if unveiling a piece of art.

Saira started to smile. This new world felt rather calm. "So, I'm a fish here?" she asked before seeing her bright silvery fins. "Oh — I guess so... But how can I live? I mean, we're not in the water?"

Mother Eagle laughed. "Oh, you have so much to learn about Echuca. Do you remember what Echuca means?"

Saira shook her head.

"Hmmbbbaaa. Meeting of the waters, my dear. Forget everything you know about how animals and plants thrive on earth, because here, in Echuca, things are different. Even fish like you can walk here."

"Wow. Cool," said Saira, standing up. Sure enough, she was balancing quite well on her square, silver-coloured tail. "So, what now then? The purple liquid?"

"We have to take it from the Tree of Life," explained Mother Eagle.

"That's a cedar tree, right?"

"Great! You remember that much," said Mother Eagle, her beak bending upwards into a grin. "But not just *any* cedar tree. The Master Tree of Life. That's the one that produces the purple tonic you need."

Saira nodded.

"It's just up the way. You might recognize the area when we get there."

The two forged through the forest walking along on their talons and tail. Along the way, Saira still had the feeling they were being followed. But every time she turned around, she saw no one. She once swore she could see two black circles staring at her through the trees, but when she blinked again, they were gone.

Saira and Mother Eagle arrived at a clearing. Before them stood the largest cedar tree she had ever seen. The trunk was so wide it could hold a house and garage, and she couldn't even see the top of the tree. There were only speckles of blue sky and clouds cutting through the tiny gaps in the enormous branches.

"Is this supposed to be familiar?" asked Saira, looking to Mother Eagle.

"Hmmbbbaaa. I guess the grandeur is obstructing your view, so to say," responded Mother Eagle, motioning for her to turn around.

Saira looked puzzled. She walked to the left of the tree and could see a large hill covered in mounds of heavy moss and grass as high as a fence. Then, she saw a door made of animal skin. "Ah! I'kinuxw's house! But wait. I thought there were no human forms here?"

Mother Eagle's beak curved up once more. "Hmmbbbaaa. I had to make a little private space for myself, that's all."

The two walked through the door flap and into the tree trunk's hollow middle. Saira sat down and looked from side to side. They were sitting in the same place she had been with Wamta only days earlier, and yet it was different. Very different. She could see massive beetles and spiders creeping everywhere and many empty viles, just like the one she had received from I'kinuxw.

Mother Eagle went over to a small stick protruding perpendicularly from the trunk. She placed her beak around it and twisted four times clockwise. She then took out a small vile from her wing and waited. Within seconds, Saira heard a slow dripping sound. *Plink. Plink. Plink.* A viscose purple liquid was falling into the vile. It was just like tapping a maple tree at Christmas in Montreal. Saira watched intently as the liquid rose to the top. Then, Mother Eagle turned the stick back four times to the right. When the plinking stopped, she extended her wing.

"Ok, so what will this *actually* do to me?" said Saira, taking the small vile in both her hands.

"Hmmbbbaa. Please, Saira, sit," said Mother Earth, pointing to a patch of moss. Saira took a seat. An enormous worm, the size a snake, scurried from under her knee. "Your powers allow you to tap into the world of animal spirits and time travel," Mother Earth began. "But like everything, there are rules. You cannot time travel anywhere or anytime, nor with *any* animal. You will learn what spirits you can tap into, depending on the culture. But here, in First Nations culture, as you know, you've tapped into the salmon spirit. This is a very important animal in Indigenous culture and your uncle Wakes passed his knowledge to you."

"*Uncle* Wakes?" repeated Saira.

Mother Eagle affirmed. "You'll understand soon enough. It's not for me to explain. The point is that here in Puntledge, or Coast Salish territory, every time you touch an object with the same frog and salmon crest carved into cedarwood you time travel."

This much made sense to Saira.

"But — and this is *very* important — once you've entered a specific time period for the first time, you have set this as your starting point. And from here you can only travel in one direction. Otherwise, it breeds too much evil."

Saira wrinkled her brows.

"What this means is you cannot jump around in the past. No hopscotching across time periods. For example, if you arrived in June 1941, you cannot go back to May 1941."

Saira was thinking about the global hopscotch game she and Grandpapa played. Mother Eagle continued. "Now, the problem is that sometimes newcomers, like yourself, make silly mistakes that – for first time travellers – we correct. Like you interfering in this latest episode, hmmbbbaaa, which has meant that you, well... *you* will never exist in the earthly form." There was a long pause while Saira tried to understand. She still didn't get why she wouldn't exist. "As a one-time act only, we are allowing you to go back and change the error," said Mother Earth, her tone firm. "But this is a one-time act. *Only,*" she repeated.

Saira quickly acknowledged.

"I know you still have many questions," Mother Earth continued. She pointed her beak towards the ground. "Your uncle had to make a very difficult decision, Saira and I think it's best that he explains that to you himself. He still has the scar above his eyebrow — you may have noticed — like you. Though his powers are no longer. That was his sacrifice... Hmmbbbaa. We shouldn't waste any more time. If you agree, go ahead and drink the liquid."

Saira stared at the iridescent purple liquid in her hands. *How could such a small bit of liquid hold such incredible powers?* she wondered. *What if it kills me?* She looked up at Mother Earth. All she could hear was the sound of her heartbeat. She let out an enormous sigh, then shot back the contents of the vile.

CHAPTER 18

Saira woke to the familiar smell of cedar. Above her, she could see the sky darken as clouds were closing in and rain started to pour down. She watched as the treetops began to dance in the wind and water droplets sprung off the branches like tiny bouncing balls. She was laying on a large patch of moss, but it wasn't the thick duvet of moss she had sat on in Echuca. The ants that began scurrying over her kneecaps were also the size of rice grains. She let out a deep exhale. *I must have made it back to the past world.*

As she stood up, she wasn't sure which direction to go. Then she heard a familiar whirling sound, followed by a hummingbird's needlepoint beak as it came whirling past her nose. "Wow, this really is a replay," she whispered under her breath. She put out her index finger, just as she had done before. Sure enough, the bird fearlessly landed on the tip. And then, exactly on cue, a raven cawed from the treetops above, sending the hummingbird scurrying off. Saira's heart started to pick up pace. The sound of muffled voices came from off in the trees. "Come…safe…together."

Saira got down and shimmied across the wet ground towards the large cedar tree. She could see the same two people standing a few metres away — one was tall, wearing dark clothing. This time, though, Saira didn't dare move. A few seconds later, she watched the small frog – the very one that had initially jumped across her face. Then, the bottom pant legs of this unknown person and Wamta's moccasins walked closer together. Saira turned her head to the left. She could see behind the large black boots.

They were standing just a few metres off, under another cedar tree. Saira waited, breathing very slowly. It felt like eternity. The leaves on the fern made a soft crinkling sound. The snake that had previously slid its way up her calf slithered by, oblivious to Saira. "Unbelievable," she whispered to herself. "This is all playing out exactly as it did before…" But this time, rather than her screaming and running out onto the path, Saira didn't budge. She just watched. The black boots began to trudge through the mud towards Wamta and this third, mystery, person. Saira arched her neck, trying to catch a better look. Finally, a light wind blew just enough leaves from the huckleberry bush that she could see the outline of a bucket hat on the much taller figure. She strained to see more, but a much larger cedar tree blocked her view. With their heads turned away and the rain falling even harder, Saira could barely hear what they were saying. Wamta's voice sounded afraid. The third person's voice was calm and pleading. It sounded like a boy. It was next to impossible to hear the third person.

Saira leaned in a bit further to see what was happening. It was so hard not to run out to save Wamta. *This is a one-time act only,* she recalled Mother Eagle's voice. *If you interfere with the past you won't exist in the present…* Saira swallowed hard. She had to restrain herself. She must stay put.

Finally, she could make out what must have been Wamta's left hand. At the end of her wrist was the colourful thread friendship bracelet. She was placing her hand – willingly, it seemed – in the younger boy's hand. She then extended her right hand and hesitantly placed it in the other person's palm. This other person had much bigger fingers. Saira twisted her head, trying to see more. Then came a loud crack, followed by three huge swirls of smoke that curled their way up through the wet trees and disappeared into the stormy sky.

For at least a minute, Saira just watched as the last bits of smoke faded into the air. Raindrops continued to fall, hitting her on the cheeks, chin and eyelids. She was shocked by what she'd just seen. She began wiping away the water, like tears from her face. *Who was that other person? Why did they take Wamta and how did they take her? Will I ever see her again?* Saira's thoughts were whirling.

The forest suddenly became very still. The rain stopped falling. The wind stopped blowing. And the insects stopped buzzing. There were no rustling reptiles, nor shaking tree branches. Saira began to feel very, very alone. Not only was Wamta gone, but Saira was now in the past world without her friend and she had no sure way of getting back to the present. *What a crazy mess! How do I know I'll get back to the present? I never should have taken that purple liquid. Why did I trust Mother Eagle to begin with!*

Saira fell to the ground. She was exhausted and scared. It was nearly night and she'd have to get out of the forest before it got too dark. She closed her eyes to think. When she reopened them, the small hummingbird she'd seen earlier was staring directly back at her. Saira let out a little smile as she watched it hover in front of her nose.

"Cute little thing, hmmbbbaaa?" said a voice behind her.

"Oh! You startled me!" cried Saira. But the hummingbird remained whirling in front of her nose.

"I guess you haven't officially met, but this seems as good an introduction as any," gestured Mother Eagle towards the hummingbird.

"Excuse me? You're talking about this?" asked Saira, now looking cross-eyed at the bird.

"Do you remember Kwa'ak'wamt'a's spirit animal," asked Mother Eagle. Her head was tilted to the side.

Saira paused to think. "A hummingbird? Oh wow! Is this — wait a minute. Is this *Wamta?*"

Mother Eagle let out a tiny giggle. "Hmmbbbaaa. It's her animal spirit."

Saira was confused. "Will I — will I ever see her again?" she started. "I mean, in the *human* form?" The hummingbird whirled faster around her head.

Mother Eagle offered a gentle smile. "Would you like to?"

"Definitely," said Saira. "I have so many, many questions. But really, I just want her to know that I miss her. She's, like, become one of my best friends. Will I be able to go back to the present, Mother Eagle?"

"Would you like that?"

Saira bobbed her head.

"Hmmbbbaaa. I must tell you something important though," said Mother Eagle, her tone turning serious. "Just remember that not everyone has your gift. I advise against speaking to anyone — except those who know — about what you've witnessed or experienced."

Saira didn't understand. "Those who *know*? How will I know who I can talk to? Can I talk to Wamta?"

Mother Eagle just shook her head. "Are you ready to go back?" she asked, stretching out her wing.

Saira looked at the long, speckled feathers. She knew that by going back she'd have a very big secret to keep. "Ok," she whispered.

"Hold on, hmmbbbaa," said Mother Eagle as she began fluffing up her feathers. "Here... we... goooooo!"

When Saira woke she was sitting in the dark, her back leaning against the bed in her room at Grandpapa's. Her temples ached. All this time travel was making her tired. She turned to the side and felt relieved when she bumped against the corner of the bedside table. She switched on the reading lamp and let out a huge sigh when she saw the familiar sight of Grandpapa's bedspread and the dreamcatcher next to her pillow. *Thank goodness. I really made it back again. Or... wait a minute! Did I, maybe, dream all of this?*

She began to doubt everything. All of her last adventures with Mother Eagle, Echuca, even the time travels. She felt her pant pocket for the photograph, pulling it out. It was the very same photo she'd first taken from Grandpapa's box. The photo with Grandpapa and two kids on either side.

Saira let out another deep breath, then looked up. The side of her backpack was peeking out from the back of the closet. Remembering the unread letter from her mom, she reached up and grabbed it. The corners of the red envelope were now slightly bent. She paused for a moment running her finger over her name that was neatly handwritten across the front. She flipped the envelope over. Her mother had sketched the design of a frog with its tongue extending into the mouth of a salmon. "Woah!" Saira said under her breath, before gently tugging it open.

The letter was written on a single sheet of rice paper. There was something wrapped up inside. When she saw it, the hairs on her forearm stood on end. There in her hands, neatly pressed between the translucent stationary, was the colourful thread friendship bracelet she'd given to Wamta.

———— ◦ ————

The sound of her phone ringing brought her back to reality. It was Nakawe. She'd missed four calls from her already.

"Chica, what's going on? Where have you been?" cried Nakawe into the phone. "I've been trying to get ahold of you! I wasn't sure if you were able to travel back again and was getting so worried. You know the photo you sent me, well I zoomed in. It looks like your friend Wamta is actually wearing my bracelet, you know the one you gave her."

"Really?" said Saira, her voice hollow. "I — I actually didn't notice the bracelet," she continued reaching for the photograph again. She paused for a moment then continued. "Nak, this situation…this time travel and Wamta stuff… it's —it's actually become a whole lot more complicated since we last spoke."

"What do you mean?" asked Nakawe.

Saira looked down at the photograph again trying to think of the right words. But as she did, she began looking more closely at the photo. Nakawe was right. Sure enough, there on Wamta's left wrist was the very same friendship bracelet she'd given her after the canoe race. She looked over at Grandpapa and Wakes. "Oh!"

"What? What's going on?" asked Nakawe, her face pressed up against her phone.

"Nak. Sorry. I have to check something. Hang on a sec." Saira put Nakawe on speaker phone and went back to the closet. She began rummaging through the top shelf before finally retrieving the pillowcase, along with her small collection of time travel objects: the leather notebook, wooden bowl and Talking Stick. She had no idea what happened to the wooden plate she'd received from Wamta's mom. Maybe it disappeared when she travelled back into the future where she no longer existed? She found the sash from Grandpapa and sat back down by the bed. In one hand she held the sash, in the other the photograph.

"What are you doing?" asked Nakawe.

"Sec," whispered Saira, looking back and forth at the sash in her hands and the sash on Grandpapa's bucket hat in the photograph. "Unbelievable," she continued nodding her head. Both designs were identical. The only difference was that the sash in her hands was more worn and had a small tear on the side. "Nakawe," Saira started. "This is wild, but my Grandpapa… I believe my Grandpapa took Wamta and her brother from the past into the future."

Nakawe just stared through the phone.

"But not only that…" Saira continued biting the side of her bottom lip, "Wamta's brother… he's — he's actually Tooan, my Grandpapa's helper."

"Huh? What! This is crazy," said Nakawe.

Saira was now pointing to the picture of the boy in the photo. "See, the scar? It cuts through his left eyebrow. That's the exact same scar Tooan has."

"Are you sure?" asked Nakawe, squinting at the phone.

"Oh wait," continued Saira, ignoring Nakawe's question. The pieces of the puzzle were falling into place. "I almost forgot, but Satsam told me his Dad changed his name when he married! He married a Cherokee wife... he didn't tell me what his first name was, but I know he changed it to Tooan-tuh because it also means frog!"

Nakawe just looked at Saira and shook her head from side to side.

"Nak, I'm sure of this," continued Saira, her voice gaining energy. "The boy in the photograph —Wakes, Tooan, or whatever we want to call him — it's the same person. When I showed Wamta the photo, she confirmed that it was her brother. And I know this is also the same person that works with my Grandpapa. They have the same jet-black hair, big eyes and olive complexion. I'm absolutely sure of it!"

Nakawe was still speechless.

"This also means... that Tooan, or Wakes, is... well... he's my *uncle*," Saira continued.

"Chica, you've totally lost me now. What do you mean your uncle? Are you going loca?"

Saira held the friendship bracelet up to the phone so Nakawe could see it.

"Oh. My. God." whispered Nakawe. "How—? Why—?"

"Nak, I've got to call you back. There's something I think I should read first."

<hr />

Saira carefully pulled open the letter and sat down on her bed, the dreamcatcher laid on the bedside table next to her. She started reading.

Dear Saira,

Maybe you'll read this on the plane, or perhaps you'll wait until you're at Grandpapa's, staying in my old room. Either way, I wanted to send you a little note while you're away.

We know it's been very hard for you these last few months, Saira. Your Dad and I wanted to protect you, but you're a big girl now. You're old enough to understand.

As we get older, we change in all sorts of ways. Sometimes we open ourselves to new adventures, people and place. Other times we want to go back in time, press pause and seek the familiar as comfort.

Unfortunately, people — even those we love and keep closest — don't always change alongside or in the ways that we hope. This is OK. It's a part of life. Your Dad and I always love you. We don't need to be together to do that.

Maybe one day soon you'll understand that families are not always who or what we think they are. Sometimes the bonds between people go beyond time and place, whether they come from the same blood or not. Other times, people of the same blood have trouble connecting. The importance is in knowing where you come from, so you can know where to go.

I wish I had better memories of my own childhood, but I don't. I think losing my mom at such a young age made me forget many things. But I did meet a very special friend when I was about your age. You would have liked her. She was kind and curious, well ahead of her time. She gave me this friendship bracelet that I'm now giving to you. It will remind you that you're never alone. As she said to me: "Colourful threads of

love both protect and reveal". I hope they do both for
you, sweetie. Love always. xo Mom

By the time Saira finished reading the letter, tears were falling.
She suddenly understood why she never knew anything about her
mom's childhood and why she'd never seen any photos of her as a
young child. Her mom probably didn't know anything herself! But
she still had so many unanswered questions. Why did Grandpapa
take her mom and Tooan? Where was her Grandmother? And, most
importantly, how much did her mom and Tooan actually know
about what happened to them?

That night Saira barely slept. Her mom was arriving the next
day. She needed answers to her questions, but she remembered
Mother Eagle's words: *"… not everyone has your gift. I advise against
speaking to anyone — except those who know — about what you've
witnessed or experienced…"*

But how would she know who to talk to?

CHAPTER 19

When Saira fell asleep that night she dreamt she was back in Echuca. The familiar scent of fresh grass and flowers seeped into her nose. Her arms and legs were now a salmon body and she was laying on one of her fins outside on a tall bed of grass. Her square, silver-coloured tail flapped up and down on the long, green blades. The gurgling sounds of a nearby brook rumbled in her ears and, as she lifted her head, she looked straight into two stark brown circles.

Smiling down at her from his perch, on an enormous overturned cedar tree, was a giant, green frog. "Well, hello there, Saira!" said Wakes, his big eyes bulging. "Took you awhile."

"Wakes?" asked Saira wearily. "Is that you?"

"It's not exactly your prince charming now, is it?" he replied snorting with laughter as he bounced towards Saira.

She forced a smile.

"I bet you have some questions for us all, now don't you?" he continued resting a webbed hand on Saira's fin.

She nodded.

"You realize we're family now, so I can share a few things," Wakes started, before turning his eyeballs round to see that no one was around. "As Mother Eagle told you, I can explain many things to you, but best we speak in our earthly forms."

"Um, ok," whispered Saira. "But why? I mean, what difference does it make?"

"It's easier to talk in privacy, without the other animals around. 'Never know who's listening with their owl ears and eagle eyes...'"

"But can you just tell me one thing?"

Wakes stood expressionless.

"Are you —?" she started. "Are you... *Tooan*? And are you my... my *uncle*?"

Wakes smiled then blinked hard as if he were nodding with his eyes.

"Wow. Ok," said Saira. "I guess we'll talk more back home, then? I have just so many things I don't understand... you, my Grandpapa, my mom..." Just then, the small hummingbird she'd seen in the past world whirled between her and Wakes. The bird fluttered in place for a few moments, then sped off.

"Remember what Mother Eagle told you. Not everyone is in touch with their animal spirit," he said, pointing his flat nose in the direction of the hummingbird. "You are one of the very few. Well, like me... But to answer your question, yes, we'll speak soon, dear one. Tomorrow, meet me under the golden cedar tree at the trickster raven's nest in the morning."

"The trickster raven's nest?" Saira repeated.

"That's riiiiiight!" And with that, Wakes took an enormous leap off the grass, hurtling up into the crystal blue sky.

In the morning, Saira woke to the rumble of Grandpapa's car pulling up the driveway and a couple of doors slam shut. Her heart jumped when she heard the familiar sound of her mom's voice as she and Grandpapa walked up the back porch. She leaned over to the bedside table and grabbed the thread bracelet. What will she say to her mom now that she knows she's actually Wamta? And what about Wakes and her latest dream? She needed to speak to Tooan, and fast. But how would she talk to him in private? Saira looked over at her phone. Nakawe had texted in the night: *Thinking of u chica. Let's talk soon!*

Saira was too anxious to reply. She picked up the thread bracelet and carefully slid it round and round on her wrist. She stared at it for a few moments, twirling the strings in her fingers. It still fit perfectly. She threw on her housecoat and headed down the stairs.

The sound of Grandpapa coughing from the kitchen made her uneasy. Seated at the table was Tooan, her mom and Grandpapa. They had uneaten bowls of yoghurt and granola in front of them and were slowly sipping liquorice and nettle tea. The atmosphere felt strange. *Why wasn't anyone talking?* When they saw Saira, all three leapt up.

Her mom threw her arms out wide. "Sweetie! How are you? What happened to your eyebrow?"

Saira almost forgot she had this cut, which was already becoming a faint scar just like Tooan's. "Mom, I'm so happy to see you," Saira cried, reaching out to her. "It's fine. Just a small accident, that's all," she continued, nestling her face into her mom's side.

"Morning, Saira," said Tooan and Grandpapa in unison. They both looked down at their tea while Saira and her mom hugged.

"Sleep ok, my little traveller?" asked Grandpapa after a moment.

"Yah sure, Grandpapa."

"Ah, Saira? I was going to go…get some berries for our granola and yoghurt. Want to join?" asked Tooan.

Saira looked up and stared straight into Tooan's deep brown eyes. Her arms tingled. It was like looking at Wakes in her dreams. "Yes. Yes, I do," she answered, heading for the door.

The two walked in silence down Grandpapa's driveway. They were headed towards the golden cedar tree with its outstretched branches. Once there, Tooan passed Saira a small wooden bowl for collecting berries. She reached out her hands, then immediately froze. On the side of the bowl she could see the now familiar design of a frog with its tongue extended down to a salmon. She threw back her hands and stepped back.

"It's OK, Saira," said Tooan calmly. "You can touch it now. You won't be going back there again."

——— ◆ ———

For the next few minutes, Tooan and Saira stood under the golden cedar tree. Neither looked down at the salmonberries or Oregon grape bushes, let alone picked any of them. Saira held the wooden bowl close to her chest.

"It will never go away completely, but in time it will fade…a lot," reassured Tooan lightly tracing his fingers along his own scar. "It's the only way we have of recognizing one another."

Saira still wasn't sure where to start asking questions. There were so many. "But why?" she started, her voice stammering. "I mean, why *me*…? Why my mom? Why *you*…? Why *Grandpapa*? Why *any* of this?"

Tooan rested his hand on Saira's shoulder. He took in a long, deep breath. "Many years ago, your grandpapa had a tough choice to make," he began. "When Petah, his wife — your grandmother — got sick, he was desperate to help her. All the medical doctors told him she was going to die. But he refused to believe them. He wanted to do whatever was in his power to save her."

"Wait a minute," interrupted Saira. "You're talking about Petah, like Wamta's baby sister Petah? Oh my gosh. I just realized. That's… that's my *grandmother*?" Her mouth dropped.

"That's right." Tooan looked off into the distance, towards the bay, before continuing. "When your grandpapa was in the Amazon, in Brazil — this was before your grandma got sick — he received some magic stones from the Yagua Shamans."

Saira remembered Grandpapa telling her this.

"When your grandpapa was there, he learned that these stones had time travel powers. They still worked back then, and Shamans often used it for medicinal purposes. But, of course, your grandpapa refused to believe any of it —in the beginning that is. He just

146

stored the stones away in a box, part of his cultural anthropology collection, and almost forgot about them altogether. But then, after your grandma got sick, he was so desperate. He eventually turned to witch doctors for help. He returned to see the Yagua Shamans.

Saira was still unsure at how or why this involved Tooan or her mom. "So, why did he take *you*?

"They told him that the only way Grandpapa's wife could possibly survive was if he could get a Shaman from her own family — someone with the same DNA — to make her medicine," Tooan continued. "That's pretty hard to find, to be honest. Obviously not every family has a Shaman. In fact, it's usually genetic and you'll find many along the same family line. But in our case, she was lucky... in a way. That person, that Shaman family member... that was me."

"*You* are a Shaman?" Saira asked.

"At the time I was only dabbling in it. I didn't really know who I was. I was just a kid – about your age. I knew I had some special powers and had very strange animal dreams, but I had no idea how far my abilities could take me. This all happened about the time I started at residential school too, so I was only able to start working with I'kinuxw whenever I came home for the summer months. It actually saved me. It was the only way for me to secretly keep part of my culture."

"Wow," said Saira, hanging on his every word. "And, Grandpapa? He came to take you away? To help cure Grandma?"

"That's right, Saira. He thought I'd be able to help. And really, I tried. I did. I wanted as much as he did to save my baby sister's life. I'd have done anything for her. But..." Tooan's voice trailed off. "I — I just wasn't able to."

Saira put her hand on his arm.

"As you can imagine, your grandpapa was so upset. He, too, would have done anything for your grandma. Once she passed, he asked if I'd stay and work with him. I felt so badly for what happened...we were both mourning I guess...so I eventually agreed. We travelled the world. We were a team. Though he was the well-known anthropologist, as you know. I was his 'helper'. But I helped him cure hundreds of people from around the world."

Saira was silent for a few moments, letting this all sink in. There was so much to understand. "But why…? Why could you cure them — these other people — but not Grandma?"

"Honestly, I don't know. I guess there are just some things we can never explain. And that, well, that is… unfortunately, one of them."

Saira was quiet again. The wheels in her brain were spinning. "Why didn't you go back to the past to live again? Why did you decide to take my mom into the future?"

"This was another difficult choice…Gosh, isn't life full of them?" Tooan let out a slight smile, then clasped his hands together. "I needed to make a sacrifice for the benefit of someone else in my family. Your mom — Wamta — was supposed to go to residential school. I believe she told you in the past world. And as I had already been there, I knew how awful it was; how much suffering we went through. It would have killed Wamta's spirit entirely. She loved school, but she also loved her culture. There was no way I was going to let her go to Port Alberni Indian School. So, I went back in time to get her. Your grandpapa came with me. He wasn't sure I had the strength to do it on my own. And then together we brought her back to the future."

"Wow," repeated Saira. "But she doesn't know *any* of this?"

Tooan shook his head. "You met Mother Eagle by now, so you know that one of the principle rules of Echuca is that you cannot jump around in the past. What you probably didn't learn yet is that if you take someone from the past into the future, like I did with your mom, you lose your time travel powers completely. And that's exactly what happened to me."

"Woah."

"But, you know, I don't regret it. Not for a second," answered Tooan. "I would never have let your mom suffer through this time period the way she would have. And, as you know by now, you wouldn't even be here today, if she had…"

"I know," said Saira quietly.

"Your mom doesn't live in both worlds — the earthly world and the spirit world— like we do. She would never be able to fully understand. Your grandpapa and I have had to keep this a secret. But now, it's up to you to decide if you want to share this with your mom or not. It's not our choice to make anymore."

Saira looked confused. "What do you mean?"

"Your grandpapa is very ill. The doctors don't know what he has exactly." Tooan was choosing his words carefully. His brown eyes were growing darker. "That's why your mom came out here. That's also why we've been hurrying to pack his stuff. We don't actually know how long he has left."

Saira looked down at her feet. Her knees were feeling weak. "Isn't there anyway to help?"

"I don't think so. It's been diagnosed as terminal," Tooan replied. "Look, I think we should head back now. I know your mom is excited to see you."

"OK," said Saira, turning back round towards the house. She was still clutching the empty wooden bowl.

As they walked back, Saira swung her head back round. She was sure she felt someone watching them. But yet again, she saw nothing. Only leaves blowing in the morning breeze. "Tooan?" she said suddenly realizing something. "If you are my uncle, then Satsam…well, then he's my cousin!"

"Haha, that's right, dear one," answered Tooan, letting out a wink and a small snort of laughter.

"Wow," said Saira, grabbing for Tooan's hand. "I've never had a cousin!"

———◆———

That evening, Saira called Nakawe to explain everything she learned.

"Unbelievable, chica," said Nakawe by the end. "I just can't believe this…You have Shamanic time travel powers to not only move through time but also through aniam!"

"It's kinda crazy, isn't it?" said Saira. "The hardest part is that my mom has no idea about any of this. I'm not even sure my Grandpapa knows how much I know. Gosh, I don't even know if I really believe all of this! It's still so new."

"Have you talked with your mom yet?"

"Not really. She and Grandpapa have been in his office most of the day. I think they're going through all his old stuff."

"Are you going to tell her what you know?" asked Nakawe, her voice rising.

"I don't know yet, Nak. I mean, maybe some things are best kept secret. You know?"

CHAPTER 20

The next day Saira, woke early. They didn't have to leave for the airport until 10am, but by 6am she was already wide awake. She grabbed the pillowcase from the back of her closet and snuck out of the house. She wanted to take one last morning walk along the bay.

Since her talk with Tooan she hadn't had any time to spend alone with either Grandpapa or her mom. She had so many mixed feelings. What she learned from Tooan was still pretty unbelievable. She decided to pretend like she knew nothing, until she was absolutely sure of what to do, if anything at all. She couldn't shake this new feeling in her belly. It was a mixture of sadness and uncertainty, but also a new sense of closeness to her mom. She was sad that Grandpapa was ill, sad to learn about all he went through to try and save his wife – her Grandma. She also felt sad that Tooan went through such suffering at residential school and that her mom would never know about any of this. But somehow Saira felt a sense of responsibility. Learning that she inherited time travel powers, like her uncle, made her feel a kind of duty to her family, a family now much larger than she ever realized. But she couldn't say exactly what she was intended to do. *What good are these powers, then?* she wondered, approaching the marshy area just before the water.

She looked up into the August morning sky. It was mostly clear with just a few puffy white clouds overhead. Queneesh looked radiant in the background, and the water, calm as glass. Strangely enough, there were no birds in sight. No ravens circling overhead. No eagles peering down from above. And certainly, no hummingbird whirling past her head. The silence felt uneasy.

She knelt down on the patch of dandelions growing alongside the salmonberry bush. She could still make out the large hole where the totem pole had been dug up a few days earlier. She put the pillowcase down and ran her hands through the dirt. She breathed in the earthy smell and enjoyed feeling the cold, wet soil under her fingernails. She couldn't help thinking back to the first time she came there with 'Wat'si. The first time she touched the totem pole and was flung back into time. Where it all began. She started digging in the hole, lifting out small mounds of soil until the hole was just big enough. She then opened the pillowcase and took out each object one-by-one: the wooden tea bowl from Wamta, 'Wakes' leather notebook and the Talking Stick from the Sharing Circle. She held each one in her hands for a few moments, turning them round and round. *I guess you've each served your purpose,* she thought to herself before saying a silent good-bye to each one. She then covered the hole with soil and placed her hands overtop the freshly padded plot. She took a deep breath in. *Gilakas'la, dear Wamta.*

<hr />

Strangely, it wasn't hard for Saira to say goodbye to Grandpapa and Tooan at the airport. She had this feeling she'd be seeing them both again soon. Though how, where and why, she had no idea. Her mom's goodbye, though, was tearful. She hugged both Tooan and Grandpapa for a very long time. Saira stood nearby, her head down, twirling the thread bracelet around on her wrist. It was unusual for her mom to be so emotional.

"See you soon, my little traveller," said Grandpapa, removing his spectacles before muffling his cough into his inner elbow. "It was fun to have you out. I hope you still have my colourful sash from global hopscotch?"

Saira tapped the back of her pack. "Sure do, Grandpapa. I'm already looking forward to our next game."

Grandpapa grinned, then ruffled the top of her hair.

"Great to finally meet you, Saira," said Tooan, stepping forward and extending his arms. "Hope we cross paths again soon."

"Thank you, Tooan. Thank you," Saira repeated, reaching in for a hug. "And please, say bye to my cuz for me," she whispered.

"Sure thing," Tooan whispered back with a wink.

Once on the plane, Saira and her mom settled into their seats. Her mom pulled out her phone to check work messages and Saira grabbed her book, *Great Animal Spirits of the Pacific Northwest*. She hadn't had a chance to read it over the last few days. There were still a few pages left.

"Enjoying the book?" asked her mom, looking up from her phone.

"Love it, Mom. It's so interesting."

"That's good, sweetie. What's your favourite animal in there?"

"Easy," said Saira, looking directly at her mom. "A hummingbird."

"Mmmm, that's nice," she replied, turning back to her phone.

"Hey, Mom? How's Dad? I mean… how are *things* with Dad?" They hadn't spoken about the divorce since they'd seen each other.

"Oh, sweetie," she said, putting down her phone for a second time. "Your Dad… well, he's fine."

"Did you guys move yet?"

Her mom turned her phone to airplane mode and placed it in the front console. "I wanted to tell you when we were with your Dad, but I supposed I can tell you now."

"Tell me what, Mom?" asked Saira, a sudden lightness filling her chest.

"Your Dad, he's moved into his new place close to McGill, just like we talked about. And I… well, I've got a new job, sweetie. You and I will be moving to Portugal for a year."

"We're what?" said Saira, dropping her book.

"Isn't it exciting? We'll be able to learn more about the country where your Grandpapa's from," explained her mom in her telephone voice.

Saira placed her hand on her scar. It was starting to feel warm.

"You'll have new places to discover and new people to meet," she continued. Her words sounded rehearsed.

Saira paused, then looked down at the colourful bracelet around her wrist. "OK, Mom. That sounds great," she said finally, reaching across for her hand. "Let's go, then. I'm ready for a new adventure." And as the plane began its ascent into the clouds, the contrails behind them twisted and turned like a salmon tail swirling in the wind.

THE END

READER'S GUIDE

The following questions include a mix of comprehension and discussion questions. They are intended to be use in either a classroom or family setting and serve as a springboard to other projects or research.

Chapter 1

1. How would you describe Saira's personality? Why?
2. Why is she going to visit Grandpapa?
3. Whose land does Grandpapa say they are on, as they drive back from the Comox airport?
4. What are the different tribal regions of Vancouver Island?
5. What is a creation story?
6. What is the story of Queneesh?
7. What does Saira notice about Tooan-tuh?
8. Name three First Nations cultural aspects mentioned in this chapter.
9. What is a pedra/piedra encantada and why does Saira have one?
10. What does Saira want to do with her magic rock?
11. What animals did Saira see on the beach when she went berrypicking at Kye Bay a few years ago?

1. Learn three unique cultural aspects about *another* First Nations group.
2. Learn the names of at least three other First Nations (of the 50) that live on Vancouver Island.
3. Learn and share another creation story.

Chapter 2

1. What does Saira dream?
2. Who does she see in her dream?
3. What does Nakawe tell Saira to use to waken the spirits?
4. Why is Saira worried about Grandpapa?
5. What do you know about Grandpapa?
6. Why does Grandpapa call Saira his 'little traveller'?
7. What does Saira see when she looks outside the window?
8. What is 'explosion jam' and why is it special?
9. What does Saira know about her late grandma?
10. What is the name of Tooan's dog?
11. Why is he called this?

Research

1. Learn three different types of foods traditionally eaten by an Indigenous group.
2. Learn the significance of smudge sticks and what they are used for.

Chapter 3

1. Where is Saira when she wakes up from her fall?
2. What are the first things she notices about her new environment?

3. Where does Wamta say Saira is?
4. What does the word "potlatch" mean? In what language?
5. Why are they having a Celebration of Life ceremony?
6. What two Indigenous languages does Wamta speak?
7. What creature comes onto the dance floor? (two names)
8. Why is Wamta confused when she sees Saira's phone?
9. What is different about Queneesh glacier?
10. What year does Wamta say it is?
11. How does Wamta know English?

Research

1. Why were potlatches banned?
2. Research traditional fishing methods among the First Nations.
3. Research four facts about residential schools.

Chapter 4

1. What object does Saira carry into the present?
2. What animals and insects does Saira hear making strange noises?
3. What are Tooan and Satsam doing when Saira sees them?
4. What is an 'ania'?
5. Does Nakawe believe Saira time travelled?
6. What does Nakawe say she should do?
7. What design does Saira see on the wooden bowl?
8. What does Saira learn about the First Nations and the natural world from Grandpapa's book?
9. What does Satsam say when he sees Saira reading her book?
10. What does Saira find inside Grandpapa's office (name five things)?
11. What is written inside the leather notebook?
12. What does 'animist belief' mean?

Research

1. Research the meaning of one Coast Salish or Kwakiutl animal crest.
2. Research the Wild Woman of the Woods and share three things you learn.
3. Research pedra/piedra encantada and share two things you learn.

Chapter 5

1. Summarize Saira's latest dream.
2. What does Saira learn about her grandma?
3. How does Granpapa react when Saira asks about his "kids"?
4. What does Satsam's name mean? In what language?
5. What more do you learn about Saira in this chapter?
6. How does Satsam say his dad got the scar in his eyebrow?
7. What does Tooan-tuh mean and in what language?
8. What are two poisonous flowers Satsam shows Saira?
9. What does Saira say that impresses Satsam? Why is he impressed?
10. What does Saira touch before she time travels again?

Research

1. What Indigenous name would you like? Why?
2. Do you believe Saira's stone is magic? Why or why not?
3. Which is your favourite character so far? Why?

Chapter 6

1. What do you remember about the totem pole design that Saira sees in the past world?

2. Where does Wamta invite Saira? Why?
3. What does Wamta do on the ground, just outside the forest?
4. How many words do they have in Kwak'wala for cedar tree? Why do you think they have so many words?
5. What does Wamta call her 'special tree'? Why?
6. What does Saira tell Wamta while they are under her special tree? How does Wamta react?
7. What does Saira learn about Wamta's brother?
8. What happened when Wamta's brother went away to residential school?
9. What dome structure do the girls find during their walk? What is this place used for?
10. What is the Kwak'wala word for Shaman or spirit doctor?
11. What does Saira realize as they are headed home?

Research

1. What was residential school? Share three things you learn.
2. Do you believe in spirit doctors? Why or why not?

Chapter 7

1. Why is Wamta's mom worried about her baby?
2. What does 'Gilakas'la' mean? In what language?
3. What does 'Kwa'layu' mean? In what language?
4. Why does Wamta suggest they go see I'kinuxw?
5. What does Wamta show Saira before they leave? Why is it important?
6. How does Saira feel when they arrive at I'kinuxw's?
7. What are some items Saira sees inside his hut?
8. What do you think I'kinuxw's words to Saira mean?
9. What do you think I'kinuxw's spirit animal is? Why?

10. What is Wamta's spirit animal? Do you think this is a good animal for her?
11. What was Wamta's brother's spirit animal? What characteristics was he said to have?

Research

1. Research Bentwood boxes and share what you learn.
2. What are the personality traits of someone with an eagle animal spirit?
3. What animal spirit would you like to be? Why?

Chapter 8

1. Why is Saira surprised that she made it back to the present world?
2. What object does she bring back from the past world? What is unique about this item?
3. What does Saira find in her pocket?
4. What does the word 'kikw' mean? In what language?
5. Why is Satsam surprised to see the totem pole here?
6. What does Saira see around Satsam's neck? Where did Satsam say he got it?

Research

1. Learn three things about totem poles and share your findings.

Chapter 9

1. What does Grandpapa tell Saira when she says Satsam stole her magic rock?
2. What else does Grandpapa tell Saira that surprises her?

3. How does Saira react when Nakawe confirms what both Grandpapa and Satsam say?
4. What does Saira realize she forgot in the past word?
5. What three items does Saira take from the back of her closet?
6. What item falls out of the closet that surprises Saira?
7. Name three things Saira finds in the leather notebook.

Research

1. Share your thoughts on the magic rock. Do you think Satsam took it or did he get it from his Dad?
2. Research and share three facts about the Sierra Madre Mountains of Mexico.

Chapter 10

1. What happens in Saira's dream?
2. Why do you think the water in her dream is purple?
3. What does Grandpapa give Saira?
4. Why does Saira go back to the room where Tooan was packing boxes?
5. What does she find there?
6. How does Tooan react when he finds Saira?
7. What does Nakawe send Saira by phone?
8. What did Saira learn about Nakawe's Yaqui culture through the Easter festival?
9. What did Saira's mom tell her about living in different places at the same time?
10. What happens as Saira watches the eagle?
11. What does Saira see that surprises her?

Research

1. Would you like to live in different places at the same time? Why or why not?
2. Research animals in Yaqui culture and share what you learn.

Chapter 11

1. What does Saira witness in the sky just above where the totem pole used to be?
2. What does the eagle leave behind for Saira?
3. Why does Saira spy on Tooan and Satsam?
4. What is Grandpapa's reaction when he sees her?
5. What does Saira decide she must do?
6. What is strange about the garden?
7. What does Saira find?
8. Why do you think Saira gets strange sensations when she touches certain objects?

Research

1. Learn and share three facts about white ravens.
2. Research the meaning of eagles in Indigenous Northwest culture.

Chapter 12

1. What do you think Saira is holding when she arrives in the past world?
2. What is Wamta painting and why?
3. Why is the canoe special, according to Wamta?
4. What type of mask does Wamta put on, once in the canoe?
5. What is a 'Zodiac sign' and what sign is Saira?
6. What song do they sing on the canoe? Why is this important?

7. What happens when Saira falls overboard?
8. What is the frog's name? What does it mean?
9. What message does he bring?
10. What falls from the sky and lands next to Saira?
11. What wish does she make? Does she only make one?

<u>Research</u>

1. Research the name of two other animals in a local Indigenous language. (Use the First Voices website to help)
2. Research two more facts about frogs in the spirit world mythology of Indigenous Northwest culture.
3. Research your own Zodiac sign and share some characteristics.

Chapter 13

1. Why does Wamta give Saira a cold cloth?
2. What else does she give Saira?
3. What does Saira give Wamta in return? What does Wamta like about this gift?
4. What do the girls make and eat for breakfast?
5. Where does Wamta invite Saira?
6. What topics do they discuss at the Talking Circle?
7. Why does Wamta start crying?
8. What does Saira touch before she time travels?

<u>Research</u>

1. Research the origins of the Talking Circle or Dream Catchers, or both.

Chapter 14

1. What does Saira bring back to the present world?
2. What three objects from the past does Saira now have with her in the present?
3. What happens to Saira that night?
4. What does Mother Eagle tell Saira about her ability?
5. Where on Saira's body is evidence that she "has been marked"?
6. What does Mother Eagle say about the animal spirits and objects?
7. Who does Nakawe show Saira's photo to?
8. What are the reactions of Grandpapa and Tooan to Saira's cut?
9. What does Saira see in the open box?
10. How does she react?

Research

1. Research and share two facts about Mother Eagle.

Chapter 15

1. Who does Saira think is the girl in the photograph?
2. Who does she think are the other two people?
3. What questions does Saira have?
4. What does Saira realize about the bowl, notebook and Stick?
5. What is on the design?
6. What first shocks Nakawe when she sees Saira?
7. What idea does Nakawe have?
8. What happens just before Saira's hands touch the hard object in the garden?

Research

1. Why do you think Saira feels like someone, or something, is constantly watching or following her?
2. Research the meaning of frogs with extended tongues in Indigenous culture.

Chapter 16

1. What is Saira's time travel object, this time?
2. Where does Wamta's mother tell Saira to go to find Wamta?
3. What does Saira stop to look at, just after entering the forest? Why do you think this is important?
4. Whose voices does she hear?
5. What frightens Saira?
6. How does Wamta feel when Saira sees her?
7. What is strange about the photograph that Saira shows Wamta?
8. What does Saira touch before time travelling back to the present world?

Research

1. Research "transformation masks" and share what you learn.
2. Why do you think Wamta disappeared from the photograph?
3. Do you think the boy is Wamta's brother? Why or why not?

Chapter 17

1. Why can't Grandpapa see Saira when she arrives back in his garden?
2. What does she realize when she gets back to her room?
3. What words of caution does Mother Eagle give Saira?
4. According to Mother Eagle, what animal is Saira?

5. What does Saira learn about Mother Eagle?
6. Where does Mother Eagle take Saira? Why?
7. What does 'Echuca' mean?
8. What is strange about this place?
9. Where do they get the purple liquid from? Why is it important for Saira?
10. What does Saira learn about her family?
11. What very important time travel rule does Saira now learn?

Research

1. Research Echuca, Meeting of the Waters, and share what you learn.
2. Would you like to live in Echuca? Why or why not?

Chapter 18

1. What is different about Saira's time travel experience this time?
2. What animal does Saira manage to avoid?
3. Why is she careful not to react to the snake?
4. What does Mother Eagle say will happen if she interferes?
5. What leaves in three puffs of smoke?
6. What does Saira find inside her mom's letter?
7. What does Saira realize about the colorful sash?
8. Who does Saira finally realize is her uncle?
9. Who does Saira's mom say she got the friendship bracelet from? What does she share about this bracelet?
10. Why does Saira have trouble sleeping that night?

Research

1. Research the spirit qualities of hummingbirds in Indigenous culture. Do you think Wamta has these qualities?

2. Research an animal name in any Indigenous language that you would like to be called. Share what you learn.

Chapter 19

1. What does Saira learn about Wakes?
2. What does Wakes tell Saira about people and animal spirits?
3. What does Saira now know about Wamta and her mom?
4. What was the atmosphere when Saira walked into the kitchen?
5. Where does Tooan invite Saira?
6. Why is Saira scared to take the small wooden bowl from Tooan?
7. What does Tooan tell her about their eyebrow scars?
8. What does Saira learn about her grandmother?
9. How did Tooan time travel and why?
10. Why did Tooan and Granpapa bring Wamta with them back to the present?
11. Why doesn't Saira's mom know any of this?
12. What does Tooan explain about Grandpapa's health?
13. Who is Tooan to Saira?

Research

1. Do you think Tooan and Grandpapa made the right decision to bring Wamta into the present with them? Why or why not?
2. Do you think Saira should tell her mom what she knows or keep it a secret? Why or why not?

Chapter 20

1. How does Saira feel in the morning?
2. Why does she go back to where the totem pole was?

3. What objects does she bury?
4. Why is Saira not sad to say goodbye to Granpapa and Tooan?
5. What is Saira hopeful of when she and her mom are on the plane back to Montreal?
6. What does Saira say is her favourite animal?
7. What surprise does Saira's mom have?
8. How does Saira feel about this news?

Research

1. How would you feel if you were Saira? If you had these special powers?
2. Look back to Chapter 1: what shape were the contrails when the plane took off in Montreal? What shape are they leaving the Comox Valley? Research the meaning of snakes and of salmons in Indigenous Northwest culture.